THE CLEANER

THE MESSES SERIES, BOOK ONE

KIERSTEN MODGLIN

Cover Design by Kiersten Modglin
Formatting by Kiersten Modglin

First Print and Electronic Edition: 2018
kierstenmodglinauthor.com

To true love—the rarest and most powerful force in the universe. And to the amazing man I have the honor of experiencing it with.

ONE

GUNNER

June 2018

Gunner James was a cleaner—a crime scene cleaner, that is. He spent his days, and some nights, cleaning up the messes left behind by death. From the time his work started to the time it ended, he was surrounded by grief: devastated spouses and family members of the deceased, people whose heartbreak was so fresh you could feel it just by being near them. It always surprised him that so few people knew his job existed, that they would have to call someone like him to clean up the messes they never dreamed they'd have to. For some reason, it was a common misconception that the police were responsible for cleaning up after the bodies, making sure the family could go home without having to look at Uncle Joe's brains on the wall, but that just wasn't the case.

People were fascinated by his line of work, always asking

for pictures, details...things Gunner would just as soon not talk about off the clock. Not talk about ever, if given the choice. He hated talking about the things he'd seen. He didn't like to discuss the chemical he had to pour onto the hardwood floors to discover if any blood had seeped into the cracks; he didn't like to talk about how every time he went down the cheese aisle at the grocery store, he had to stop himself from looking around for a rotting corpse.

Gunner was good at death. He understood death. Everything about death was scientific, it could be measured. There was a process, a set of stages from the moment your heart stopped beating. And once he arrived, he had his list of tasks. There were no surprises, not if he followed all the rules. Once he was finished, if he'd done his job correctly, there'd be no sign he'd been there at all. Unlike life, death could be cleaned—erased. Death was easy. Life was where things grew complicated.

So, when he walked into his apartment building that night, at half past two, he knew what was waiting the second the scent hit him. He knew it well, the indescribable, unforgettable fragrance of a decaying body.

The halls were empty and quiet. Gunner walked up the stairs quickly, listening. He walked past his own apartment, his nose in the air as if he were a dog. The smell grew stronger as he walked down the solemn hallway. He'd grown numb to it. It had been years since the smell had made his stomach churn like it used to. He stopped in front of apartment 204, six doors down from his own. The smell was strong there, overwhelmingly so. He put his fist to the wood of the door before he could talk himself out of it, knocking cautiously. Placing his ear close to the door, he listened. There was no sign of movement, though he hadn't truly expected it. He knocked once more, a bit louder this time.

"Hello?" he called, his voice echoing down the silent hall. "Hello? Is anyone in there?" After a while, with still no signs of movement, he reached into his back pocket, pulling out an iPhone with a small crack in its screen that he'd been putting off having repaired.

Just then, he heard a door open on the floor below him. He paused, listening as someone began climbing the staircase.

"What the hell is going on up here?" His super's voice echoed up the stairwell, his short breaths labored. When he made it to the top, his hands on his portly belly, he sighed. Gunner walked toward him. "Oh, Gunner, it's just you. What are you doing? Have you any idea what time it is? You're going to wake the whole building."

Gunner pointed up, as if the smell were just above their heads. "Do you not smell that?" he asked.

"Yes, of course. I have an exterminator coming out in the morning, it was the soonest I could get someone."

"It's not a pest problem, Hermy. Someone's dead in 204."

"What?" the man asked, staring at him, and then past him toward the apartment, in disbelief.

"I'm calling the police. Someone is dead."

"No one is dead, Gunner, you're mistaken. You'll see. The exterminator will be here in the morning. It's just another animal in the walls."

"It's not an animal. You don't need an exterminator,

Hermy. You need me. But first," he paused, holding up his phone, dialing nine-one-one and placing it to his ear, "you need the cops."

WHEN THE POLICE arrived a few minutes later, Gunner saw it in their eyes. They knew it too: the smell, the look on Hermy's face—they knew what they were going to find.

"What apartment?" an officer asked.

"It's 204," Gunner responded, looking to Hermy who held out a key hesitantly.

Without another word, the officer, followed by a swarm of fellow officers and EMTs, headed up the stairs, their faces solemn.

"Hermy, you'll want to stay here." Gunner followed the officers back up the stairs, anxious to see what would be discovered. He tried to remember if he'd ever seen the face of the tenant, his neighbor, if he'd ever offered a kind word or smile as he passed them in the hallway. New York was different than where he'd grown up. You didn't know your neighbors here—didn't care to know them.

As the door to the apartment was opened, the smell surrounded him, further confirming what he'd known. No one flinched, the professionals in the hall all too familiar with the stench of death.

"Get back," one of the officers warned Gunner, but it wasn't necessary. He knew the rules. He stepped back, leaning against the wall, but trying to get a good look into the apartment.

"In here," he heard one of the officers call out and then

came the hurried footsteps. They'd located the body. He sank to the ground, sure he should go to his apartment and stay out of their way, yet he couldn't move. Some sick part of him wanted to see the body—the part of the disaster he never got to see, the maker of the messes he spent his life cleaning up.

He heard Hermy approaching him and looked his way. The man walked toward him cautiously, his mouth covered by his shirt, eyes watering. "Is she?" he asked.

Gunner nodded. "Dead. Like I told you."

"What happened?" he whispered, horrified.

"I haven't heard. They'll bring the body out soon."

He shook his head. "She was new to the city. A nice girl."

"They always are," Gunner said.

Hermy looked at him, a confused look on his face but Gunner didn't elaborate. They were always 'so nice'. He'd worked with thousands of grieving families in the seven years since he'd been working bio decontamination, and the dead were always revered. He'd never met anyone who didn't have something nice to say about the dead girl in her bed or the dead man in his rocking chair. He supposed it had something to do with the whole 'don't speak ill of the dead' thing, but also the idea that death was timeless—final. Everything horrible the dead had ever done disappeared the second their heart stopped beating and they shit themselves. Suddenly, it didn't matter so much that the pretty girl who had swallowed a bottle of pills had also created a Facebook page solely to mock an overweight classmate. In death, she was always so kind or young or innocent. Take your pick, he'd heard them all.

The man who had, in an alcoholic rage, beaten his wife

and child and then died in a drunk driving accident would be called smart and funny by all who knew him. They would say he was too soft for this cruel world. They would spew out lies about his character and no one would dare disagree because he was dead, so what did it matter anymore? Same story, different day.

After what seemed like hours of sitting in silence, waiting for the police to finish up, he finally saw the stretcher and body bag being brought up the stairs. By that time, several neighbors had woken up, poking their heads out into the hallway to see what was causing the commotion.

An officer approached them, rubbing his dark mustache. "Are you the one who called this in?" he asked Hermy.

"Me," Gunner told him, standing up. "That'd be me."

"I need to take your statement," he said, turning to address him. He pulled out a notepad and flipped it open. "How did you know there would be a body? And where to find it?"

"I smelled it the second I walked into the lobby."

"And no one else smelled it?"

"I thought we had a dead animal in the walls," Hermy said apologetically. "It wouldn't be the first time."

The officer nodded, writing something down and looking back to Gunner. "But you knew differently?"

"I knew it was human. I knew where it was and I knew it'd been there around three days in this heat, depending on the thermostat setting."

"And you knew all of this because...?" The officer looked at him, his expression suspicious.

"Because it's what I do," he said, reaching in his back pocket and pulling out his wallet.

"You're...what? A detective? A medical examiner?"

He handed the man a business card. "A biomedical cleaner," Gunner told him.

"Oh," the man said, looking over his card and jotting down his answer. "So, did you know the victim?"

"No," Gunner said. "I'm not home much. I don't know any of my neighbors."

"Except him." The officer gestured to Hermy.

"This is Hermy, my super. So, yeah, I know him."

Hermy stepped forward. "What happened to her?" he asked, his voice filled with worry.

"Do you know the victim's name?"

"Yes, of course." He nodded, putting his finger to his chin as he thought out loud. "She's new to the city. Just moved in two months ago. Heather...Hannah...no, Holly, I think." He held up his hand. "Let me go check my records." He walked away, disappearing down the stairwell.

Gunner stared at the cop. "Are you going to tell us what happened to her?"

"We don't know yet," the cop answered.

"But you have suspicions?" Gunner asked, his brow raised.

"Did you hear anything? See anything?" The officer turned the questioning back to him.

"No. The building is basically pretty quiet, but again, *I'm not home very much.*"

"Right," the officer said. "Well, okay. If you think of anything else, I trust you'll call." He handed over his own business card before waving Gunner's in the air. "This has your up-to-date contact info?"

"Of course," Gunner assured him. "I'm in apartment 214

too, if you need me." Hurried footsteps could be heard on the stairs as Gunner slid the officer's card into his pocket.

"I've got her lease here," Hermy huffed when he reached them. He held it up, flipping it over so he could see the front. "I was right. Her name was Holly. Holly Orrick. Pronounced like the vacuum, I think."

Gunner's breathing grew shallow and he looked at Hermy, ripping the papers from his hand hurriedly. His eyes darted over the lease, reading her name twice.

"What on earth?" Hermy asked, trying to take the lease back from him. Gunner looked up at the cop, his face turned stony.

"I need to amend my original statement," he said, moving the hair back from his forehead as a cool sweat began to collect. He stared at the door of her apartment, fear pounding in his chest.

"What?" the officer asked.

Without answering, Gunner barreled past the men, his chest growing tight. He couldn't move fast enough. *No. No. No. It couldn't be her.*

"Wait!" the officer yelled, trying to catch him but failing. Gunner busted into her apartment, his heart beating rapidly. She lay on the bedroom floor, half her body shielded by the black bag they'd begun placing her in. He stared her over, her dark hair pooling around her bloated and blue face. Her eyes were glassy and sunken in and foamy blood seeped out of the corner of her mouth.

He turned around, his throat tight, to face the interrogating officer. The man started to scold him but spoke softer noticing his ashen complexion. "Son, you can't be in here."

"I need to change my statement," Gunner repeated. "I knew the victim."

TWO

GUNNER

Gunner drove the interstate, his mind buzzing. Each exit was a chance for him to turn around, to change his mind—and oh, how he wanted to do just that. Eight years ago, he had sworn he'd never return to Dale, Georgia. Eight years ago, he had walked away from the town that raised him, his family and friends, and he'd sworn to never look back. And yet, the moment he'd laid his eyes on that name, he had known what would happen. The moment he'd seen her face, his path had been laid out for him. There was no choice. He was going back. He had to.

He drove across state lines, passing through New Jersey and Maryland, Virginia and North Carolina. When he arrived in South Carolina, he decided to stop for the night. It was late and he was tired; he couldn't make it much further. He pulled over in a crappy motel parking lot, climbing out of his car and stretching his legs. He took a deep breath, his lungs filling with the sweet southern air of his childhood. He started to grab a cigarette, but stopped himself. He'd been trying to quit, though, at the moment, he couldn't remember why.

He pressed the button on his key fob, hearing his doors lock before walking into the small lobby.

"Hello there." The woman at the front desk greeted him with a smile. "Checking in?"

"Yes," he said, "just for the night."

"Very well," she said, her gaze trailing over him. "Just...*one* for the night?" She looked over his shoulder, checking for another guest.

"Yes, just one." Her smile turned devious instantly, her face flushing red. A flirtatious glimmer filled her eyes. Back in New York, she would've been the type of girl he'd take up to his room without thinking. The way she stared at him, the touching of her hair—every bit of her body language told him she was waiting for an invitation, but he couldn't. There was too much going on in his brain. He just needed to shut it off for the night. He took the keycard from her hand, ignoring her skin as she brushed it against his with purpose. "Have a good night," he said, dismissing her blatant attempts.

She turned abruptly, sitting down at the computer and breaking eye contact. Her demeanor was cold now, realizing he wasn't going to react. He backed away from the counter, walking outside and up to the top floor. He walked along the narrow balcony, his hand grazing the rusty black railing until he found his room.

He sat on the bed, the smell of stale cigarette smoke filling his nose. It made him crave nicotine, but he was too tired to walk to the car again. He reached down, pulling off his shoes and flipping on the TV. After an hour had passed, he finally grew the nerve to call her. He'd been avoiding it thus far.

The phone rang twice before her groggy voice filled the line. "Momma?" he asked, his voice soft.

There was silence at first, as she inhaled sharply. "Gunner? Is that you?"

"It's me," he said.

"It's been so long..." she trailed off. "What's wrong, Gun?"

He paused, taking a breath. "I'm coming home."

THREE

GUNNER

Gunner pulled into Dale at half past ten. The sleepy town hadn't changed much since he'd seen it last—through the reflection in his rearview mirror. It was as if it had been hardly touched by his absence, a little faded, a bit more rundown, but overall as familiar as the day he left.

He stopped at the only stoplight in town, turning down his radio, and flipping on his blinker. Everything in him wanted to turn left, head to her side of town, drive past her old house. He wanted so badly to catch a glimpse of her. But he couldn't. Wouldn't. So, instead he turned right, heading for the address his mother had given him.

He drove past the tiny one-pump employee serviced gas station and the quiet old courthouse on the town square. He pulled into the gravel parking lot of the small white complex his mother had directed him to and looked for her apartment number. When he finally spied it, he slowed the car to a stop and climbed out.

The porch light flicked on in an instant. He shut his car door, running a hand through his thick, messy hair, and adjusting his rumpled clothes. His body felt stiff from the drive.

She opened the screen door, staring into the dark yard. She was smaller than the last time he'd seen her, a good thirty pounds gone. Her hair was wrapped in a dark blue bandana and even in the dark of the night he could see the wrinkles that had formed around her mouth and eyes. The eight years since he'd last seen her hadn't been kind.

"Momma?" he said her name, staring at the woman he hardly recognized in her long, white nightgown.

She stepped forward, calling out to him in the darkness. Moths buzzed around her head as she spoke. "Gunner? It's really you?"

"I told you it was me," he said, stepping onto the porch and wrapping his arms around her. She smelled the same, lavender and her favorite old perfume, yet everything about her felt different. Despite the changes, her hug was familiar, and he fell into it effortlessly. "You've lost weight."

"Yeah, well...cancer'll do that to ya."

"Cancer?" he asked, his heart falling. "What are you talking about? You never told me."

"You don't write, you don't call. I wasn't gonna call and pity-party you into coming home."

"I'm sorry," he told her honestly. "I never meant to fall out of touch."

She patted his back. "I'm fine, Gunner. Your momma's a tough old gal. I ain't going nowhere without a fight." She frowned, stepping toward the door and pulling it open. He took it from her, allowing her to enter first. "Now, get in here, we're letting all the cool air out."

He glanced around the small apartment. It was quaint, tiny knick-knacks adorning the walls. Two giant afghans covered the backs of her white couches. "This is nice, Momma," he told her.

"I see New York made you into a liar." She laughed.

"New York made me used to much smaller spaces. My whole apartment is the size of this room."

She sighed, taking his bag from him and placing it on the coffee table. "So, why are you here, Gunner? Do you need something? Is everything all right?"

"I can't pay you a visit just because?"

"*You can.* You don't. You could've done that any of the other dozen times I've asked you to come home. You've not visited in eight years and I can count the phone calls on one hand. Of course, I'm thrilled to have you home, but you'll have to understand my reservations when you show up out of the blue. I'm wondering what the catch is." She eyed him suspiciously.

He sat on one end of the couch awkwardly. "I'm sorry, Mom. I know I haven't visited. I just needed to get away from it all. After what happened—"

"I'm well aware of what happened, Gunner, because you left me here to deal with it all alone."

"Momma, please, you know I would've come home if I could," he begged her to understand, rubbing his head.

"Why are you here, Gunner? What do you need?" Her voice was harsh.

"It's not important. I haven't forgotten you just told me you have cancer."

"I've been dealing with it for five years on my own. You don't have to start worrying about me now."

"But what kind? Are you doing chemo? Radiation? You should have called."

"So should you. Now, don't change the subject. Why are you home?"

He sighed. "Holly Orrick's dead. She died in New York. And I'm the one who found her."

She sank down onto the couch next to him. "W-What?"

"I just...needed to be here. I needed to...I don't know. I don't know why I'm here. She won't want to see me. But I needed to be here."

"Does her family know?" his mother asked.

"I don't know. I gave the police the Orricks' phone number. I'm assuming they've called them by now."

"They're going to receive that news over the phone?" She clutched her heart. "You can't let that happen, Gunner." There was urgency in her voice.

"What's the alternative?" he asked, shaking his head. "And, before you say it, no. I'm not—"

"You have to," she insisted, her voice low in her throat. "You owe it to them. No one deserves to hear that over the phone. You have to tell them, Gunner. You have to go now."

"It's the middle of the night. I'm not going anywhere."

"Gunner, go," she said softly, standing up. "You go and tell that family their daughter is dead. They need to hear it from someone they know."

"It's not my place."

"Don't you dare," she said angrily. "Don't you dare let

your pride get in the way of what you know is right. You will go over there and tell that family what you know. And you will go now, if I have to drive you over there myself."

"Can't I just—"

"Now, Gunner Michael," she threatened, holding open the door. And that was that.

FOUR

GUNNER

Gunner stood outside the door of Holly's parents' house. He hadn't been up to this door in years, though he'd once spent many nights in front of it, the dim porch light buzzing and blinking, reminding him his date was over.

There was a light on in the kitchen window and he imagined Scott would be up. Gemma liked to fall asleep early, she always had. It was Scott who had remained up, waiting for them to return home from their evenings out.

He shook his head, pushing the thought out of his mind. He didn't need to go there now. Didn't need to think of her. He pressed his finger into the doorbell, waiting to hear movement. Footsteps approached the door almost immediately. He stepped back.

The dark cherry door swung open and he took a deep breath. She stood in front of him, her blonde hair pulled up in a loose ponytail. Her eyes were bloodshot, her face soaked with tears. She stared at him a moment too long, as if she'd seen a ghost.

"Gunner?" she asked, the power taken out of her voice.

"Reagan," he said, unable to catch his breath. It had been eight years since he'd seen her. Eight years since he'd spoken to the love of his life. She was every bit as beautiful as the day he'd left. Her eyes showed a sadness, a confusion, that told him what he'd feared. *They already knew.* His trip there had been pointless. His mother had been wrong.

Suddenly, interrupting his thoughts, she pressed her lips together, her face growing stern, and then the door was slammed in his face and he heard the deadbolt click.

He groaned, knocking. "Reagan, open up. I know I'm the last person you want to see right now. I just...I wanted to..." he paused, listening to the silence behind the door. His voice raised. "Oh, come on, just open the damn—"

"Gunner?" Gemma opened the door in shock.

"Mrs. Orrick. I'm so sorry. I hope I didn't wake you."

"What are you doing here, Gunner?" she asked. He tried to look over her shoulder, desperate for another glimpse of Reagan but she was nowhere to be seen.

"I'm sorry. I just...well, my mom insisted I come over. I... wanted to say I'm sorry about...well, about Holly."

Her eyes grew wide. "You're the friend?"

"Excuse me?"

She pulled him inside, shutting the door, and whisking him to the kitchen. Scott sat at the table, staring off into space. Reagan stood behind him, her stare icy as she avoided everyone's eye contact. "Scott, it was Gunner."

"What's happening?" he asked. "What was me?"

"You were the friend who identified Holly?" she asked, dropping his arm.

"Oh. Yes. It was me." He lowered his head, wishing it hadn't been.

"Why was she there? In New York? What happened? Was she with you?" Gemma asked, her eyes full of tears, begging him for answers. This part he was good at. This part he understood. It all came with the job. If he could shut off his emotions, it would be easy enough to treat this just as he would any other assignment. He turned to face her, taking hold of her shoulders.

"No, she wasn't with me. I don't know why she was in New York. I'm sorry, I wish I did. I didn't know she was there until they found her." He kept his focus on Gemma, trying to keep her calm.

"Was she...they didn't tell me how she died...they said there were no signs of trauma. What should I make of that?" she asked softly, her eyes telling Gunner she was already imagining the worst.

"I don't know," he told her, though that wasn't entirely true. "I was only there to see her for a moment. I'm sure they're still investigating."

"When will they release her body to us? We want our daughter here. We should be able to have her funeral at home," Scott said desperately, his gruff voice cracking.

"It usually doesn't take long, but I can't say anything for certain," Gunner answered, turning to face him.

"Do you think she was in pain?" Gemma asked, wiping her eyes.

"No," he said carefully, because it was just what you said at a time like this. "No, I don't think she was in any pain."

"She was supposed to be in school in Atlanta," Reagan told him. "We had no idea she was in New York."

He nodded. "I'm so sorry for your loss."

"I'm just glad you were there to find her," Gemma said. "God knows how long it would've taken for them to locate us if not. We may have...we may have never known."

"It wouldn't have taken long. You were her emergency contact on the lease," Gunner said without thinking.

"Lease?" Scott asked, all eyes suddenly on Gunner. "She was *living* there?"

Gunner looked around the room in confusion. "You really didn't know?"

They all shook their heads, horror filling their expressions. "How could we not have known where our own daughter was living? What kind of parents—" Gemma couldn't bear to finish her sentence, looking to Scott and covering her mouth.

Without an answer, Gunner remained silent. He should apologize again, but he couldn't bring himself to form the uniform phrase that was so overused in situations like this. Then again, he *was* sorry. Sorry about Holly, sorry he'd ever come there, sorry he'd ever come home.

"Look." He cleared his throat. "I'm sure you guys need some time. I just came by to express my condolences. If you need anything, I'm staying at Mom's."

"For how long?" Reagan asked, a sharpness to her tone.

"The next few days. I want to be here for the funeral."

"How kind of you," Reagan said. "Glad you could work my sister's death into your schedule."

"Reagan!" Gemma snapped, her jaw dropping.

"It's okay," Gunner told her. "Like I said, I should go."

"Thanks for coming, Gunner," Scott said, standing up and shaking his hand. "It's good to see you."

"I wish it were under better circumstances," Gunner said, nodding.

"So do I." Gemma smiled sadly, watching him turn and walk out of the house without another word.

FIVE

REAGAN

October 2008

Reagan stood in front of her locker, shuffling books around to no avail. They weren't there. She took a deep breath, trying to keep her panic at bay. She felt the warmth pooling between her legs, a sign that she was running out of time. Hopelessness began filling her mind as she weighed her options.

There was no way in hell she was walking into class like this. She took her sweater off, leaving only a small camisole, and tied the arms around her waist to cover the growing stain. She'd been sure she had extra pads left over from her last period, but she couldn't find them in her purse or her locker. The hallways were completely empty, for which she was thankful.

Of course this would happen on the one day her car was in the shop, stupid deer. *She'd rode to school with Emily that morning, but she didn't have another class with her until sixth period. She couldn't wait that long. Part of her considered going to the bathroom and waiting it out, someone who had a spare pad would have to come along at some point. But, even if she were to get lucky, she would still need to change pants and the chances of someone coming in with a spare pair of those were slim.*

Her parents wouldn't allow her to bring the new cellphone she'd gotten for her birthday to school, even though she promised to only use it for emergencies. She could go to the office, have them call her parents...but the mere thought was mortifying. Her skin crawled at the idea of facing Mr. Daniels, hot Mr. Daniels, *to tell him she had bled through her pants.*

Her house wasn't far. She sighed, realizing it was her only option. She had never skipped school before. Her parents would kill her if she got caught. But, if she could hurry, she'd only have to miss one class, two at most. No one would have to know.

She slammed her locker shut, rushing down the hallway and out the double doors.

"Dammit," a male voice whispered heatedly as the door crashed into him. She froze, knowing she'd been caught. "Watch what you're doing, would you?" he demanded.

She peered around the door, spying his long, scraggly hair and dark eyes. He glanced down at a cigarette that had fallen into a puddle, cursing at her again.

"Gunner James?" She backed up a step. "What are you doing out here? Shouldn't you be in class?"

"Shouldn't you?" he asked, sneering at her. He bent down, picking up the extinguished cigarette and shaking it off.

"That's none of your business," she said sharply.

"Agreed. So get out of here, princess." The word rolled off his tongue with venom.

"You don't have to be so rude," she snipped, turning away from him and walking through the courtyard toward the big red gate that led to her freedom. She could feel his eyes burning into her from behind.

"Wait a minute," he said, laughter in his voice. "Oh my god, are you...is Reagan Orrick actually about to attempt to skip class?" His eyes were wide when she turned back to him, as if he were witnessing a miracle...and she guessed somehow, he was.

"Shut up," she hissed, panic filling her.

"Okay, fine." He held up his hands in mock surrender, a cocky look on his face. He waited until she was standing in front of the gate, her hand held out, before he spoke up again. "But, if you're planning on leaving through there, you're going to get caught."

She turned back around. "What are you talking about?"

He smiled at her, lighting a new cigarette and inhaling a deep breath before he pointed above her head. "Smile."

She looked up, staring into a white video camera that pointed directly at her. "You asshole. Why didn't you warn me?" She jumped back out of the camera's line of vision.

"Relax. They don't monitor it unless the alarm sounds. And the alarm won't sound unless you open the gate."

"Then, how am I supposed to get out?" she asked, disliking the vulnerability in her voice.

He shrugged. "How should I know?"

"Oh, please." She scoffed. "You skip more class than you attend."

"Are you keeping tabs on me, Reagan?"

"You wish," she said, anger back in her voice. He was wasting her time and that was one thing she didn't have. She felt another gush between her legs. "Are you going to help me or not?"

"What's in it for me?" He raised an eyebrow.

"Forget it," she said, sighing. She turned, walking back toward him and the doors, accepting defeat. As she walked past him, he grabbed her arm. She looked at him, her stare icy. "Let go of me, Gunner."

"Fine," he teased, dropping her arm, "but if you want out, all you have to do is ask."

Her stare thawed, trying to decide if she should trust him. Everything in her screamed that she should run far away from him. She knew all about Gunner and the trouble he was known to cause. "Will you please help me get out of here?" she asked finally, her only hope.

He pointed to the tall brown fence behind him. "This is the only place they can't see on camera."

"How could you possibly know that?" Her eyes darted to the fence.

"Like you said, I skip more than I'm here. And, when I am here, I'm basically a wall ornament in Mr. Daniel's office. You learn a few things," he said simply.

"But how do you get out?" She looked up the metal bars, double her height.

"Climb," he told her. "I'll probably have to give you a boost."

"Oh, no. You can't," she said, embarrassment filling her as she pictured him lifting her up and seeing the mess between her legs.

"Yeah, okay. Give me some credit. You weigh like, what, ninety pounds? I think I can manage."

She frowned, recalling the scale that had read one hundred twenty-two the last time she'd checked. Without waiting for permission, he scooped her up, lifting her up to the gate. He maneuvered her feet into his hands. She leaned her weight onto the gate, hoisting a leg over. Her whole body shook with dread, but if he noticed the blood he didn't mention it. She pushed one final time, her body tumbling over the fence and she landed on the ground with a thud.

She stood up quickly, her face flushing. She dusted the grass from her knees and adjusted the straps on her tank top before looking at him again. "Thanks, Gunner," she said genuinely.

"Don't mention it, kid. Happy to corrupt you anytime," he said, a slight smile on his face. He began to walk away but stopped. "Ah, who cares?" He spun back around, running toward the gate and launching himself onto it. He threw his leg over and landed gracefully on his feet, the confidence of someone who had done this many times before.

"What are you doing?" she asked.

"I've been here too long already," he explained. "See you around, princess." He walked past her without a second look. Too tired to argue, she turned around, walking in the opposite direction. "You're just going to walk past all those windows, then?" She heard his voice behind her.

Looking ahead, she saw that this side of the building was indeed lined with several windows. "What am I supposed to do?"

"You've honestly never done this before, have you?" He looked intrigued.

"Of course not." She sighed.

"All right, look, you're talking to a master. I know all the shortcuts. Where are you parked?"

She winced. "I'm just walking home. My car isn't here today." She crossed her arms, not bothering to explain.

"You're kidding, right?"

"Why would I be?"

"You think in a town as small as Dale no one is going to notice you walking through town in the middle of a school day?" He rubbed his head as if she were frustrating him. "I can't believe I'm going to say this, but come with me." He pulled his keys out of his pockets, brushing a strand of hair from his eyes.

"What?"

"Come with me. I'll take you home."

"Why the hell would I come with you?"

"Because we probably have about two minutes before someone catches us out here. And you probably only have ten minutes before that blood on your pants seeps through your sweater, which I'm guessing isn't exactly a fashion statement. So, are you coming or not?"

She shook her head, her face burning with embarrassment. "Why are you trying to help me?"

"I guess I'm bored. Besides, I have a sister, princess." He shrugged. "Just call it my good deed for the day."

"Okay," she said softly, her body shaking, skin on fire.

He turned away from her, leading her to the back parking lot where his car sat. As she started to climb in the beat up, rusty car she looked at him, biting her lip. He reached in the backseat without a word, grabbing an old t-shirt and placing it in her seat. It was black, thankfully, and she sat down quickly, feeling another gush.

"Thank you, Gunner," she said, as they pulled out of the parking lot.

"Don't mention it," he told her. "Seriously, don't. I don't want people thinking I'm a nice guy, you know."

"Goodness no, can't have that." She rolled her eyes.

They drove through town without a word, his windows down and radio up.

"So, how come you can drive through town without anyone noticing?" she asked as they pulled onto her street.

"Well, one, I don't look like I'm twelve—"

"I don't—"

"And two, people don't care what I do."

"Of course they do," she assured him, though they both knew she was lying.

"Well, here you go," he said as he pulled up to her house, the nicest one on the street, his engine rumbling.

"Okay, I'll just be a sec. Wait here," she said, opening her car door and sliding out.

"Wait here?" he asked. "Why?"

"Aren't you going to take me back to school?"

He shook his head. "Not a chance. My good deed is done, princess. You don't cut school just to go back."

She groaned loudly, slamming his door. "Fine, I'll get back on my own." She rushed into the house, her legs squeezed together. As soon as she reached her room, she grabbed a pair of clean pants and panties and headed to the bathroom.

When she was done and had cleaned herself up, she threw on a new sweater, ran a brush through her frazzled hair, and headed back out the door. She was surprised to see his car still sitting there.

"What are you doing?" she asked, locking the door behind her.

He sighed, groaning. "I guess I'm a sucker for a princess in distress."

"Stop calling me that. I'm not a princess," she said hatefully.

"Could have fooled me." He shrugged, lighting a cigarette. "Now get in before I change my mind." She groaned, walking over to the passenger's side, moving the t-shirt out of her seat, and climbing in beside him. "You sure you want to go back to school?" he asked.

"Yes," she said firmly. "I'm not—" She stopped short, cutting off her own insult.

"You're not what?" he asked. "You're not like me?"

"I wasn't going to say that," she said, though she was lying and they both knew it.

"Yeah, we both know what you were going to say. You aren't a truant troublemaker like me," he said firmly. "You're a princess, princess. So deal with that."

She bit her lip, unsure of what to say. When they pulled into the school parking lot, she spoke again. "I don't think you're a troublemaker, Gunner."

"I am," he said simply.

"Well, maybe you are. But, what you did for me just now, it wasn't something a troublemaker would do. If you let people see this side of you every once in a while—"

"Yeah, yeah, princess, I know. If only I'd let people see the goodness in my heart." He placed a hand on his chest, feigning wonder. "Then the world could be a better place and

the sun would shine brighter and everyone would all live happily ever after."

"Why are you such a jerk?" she asked, a half-smile on her face.

"Wouldn't you like to know?" He winked, leaning toward her. She froze, waiting for his next move. His face grew closer to hers and her breathing quickened. She looked down at his lips, only inches from hers, when she suddenly heard a click. He leaned forward further, pushing her door the rest of the way open. "Now, get to class. The world just might end if you're late."

SIX

REAGAN

November 2008

Reagan stumbled through the party, feeling lighter than air. She made her way past a table of drunk jocks, ignoring their calls. She took another drink from her red cup. Suddenly, she felt a hand on her waist. He pressed up against her back, his mouth near her ear.

"Hey, pretty lady," he whispered softly.

She spun around, jerking out of his grasp. "What do you want, Isaac?"

He leaned closer to her. "Y-O-U," he said, his eyes drooping in a drunken stupor.

She pushed him back. "In your dreams," she said, scoffing. "You're drunk."

He grabbed hold of her arm. "Does it turn you on?"

"You being drunk?" She laughed.

"Me." He pulled her hand down, forcing her to feel the

semi-hardness in his pants.

She squeezed, crushing him between her fingers. He let out a yelp. "You bitch," he screamed, hands between his legs.

"Yeah, that's right. Remember that next time you think you can control this bitch." She turned, storming off to find Emily.

She walked down a long hallway, her eyes scanning the rooms in search of her friend. When she finally saw her, perched up on the bathroom counter, legs wrapped around Mark Aarons, she gasped.

"Em?" she called.

Her friend snapped to attention, her face growing red. "What's up, Rae?"

"I'm ready to go home," she said, her body growing hot.

"I'm a little busy," she said, holding her hand out to point at the boy in front of her as if Reagan couldn't see him. "Is everything all right?"

She took a deep breath, feeling a tear she hadn't been expecting fill her eyelid. "Yeah, fine. It's nothing." She turned around, rushing from the bathroom before her friend could see her cry. She rubbed her eye, brushing the tear away quickly. No way was she going to be caught crying at a party like some vulnerable little kid. She walked back to the living room where she locked eyes with Alex Donovan, his eyes narrowing at the sight of her. He was Isaac's best friend and she was sure his coming toward her couldn't be good news.

She turned around, trying to disappear into the crowd, but it was too late. "Reagan!" he called, clutching her arm. At six foot two, he towered over her.

She glanced up at him over her shoulder before facing his direction. "Yeah?"

"Can I get you another drink?" he asked.

"Um, no, thanks." Confusion filled her. He took the cup from her hands anyway, walking to the counter and grabbing the bottle of Jim Beam. "I'm drinking beer, Alex," she told him. She couldn't stand anything else.

He handed her the cup. "Beer's for pussies," he told her. "Drink the hard stuff, it'll put hair on your chest."

She took a drink, ignoring the burn and the horrible taste that filled her mouth. It was better to appease him than argue. Unlike Isaac, Alex could be dangerous. Smiling, she tapped the outside of the cup with her finger. "Well, see you around."

"Not so fast," he said, grabbing her arm again and sloshing the drink down her dress.

"Look what you did," she snapped, desperately searching for something to clean herself up with.

"Guess you'll have to take it off," he said, an evil grin filling his face.

"Screw you." She walked past him to the kitchen and grabbed a towel, wiping off her legs. She smelled like a brewery. He followed her, so close she could feel his breath on her skin. "Can I help you with something, Alex?"

"Actually, now that you mention it...I could think of a few things."

"Is that a joke?" she asked.

He put a hand on her back, pushing her forward. "Come on, let's get you something to change into."

"I'm okay. I'm just going to go," she said, feeling uneasy. The room had begun to spin.

"You aren't going anywhere, Rae. You're coming with me." Without warning, he scooped her up in his arms, heading down the hall.

"Put me down," she begged, without any power. The contents of her stomach were churning, angrily lapping at her throat. "I'm going to be sick," she said softly, not wanting to open her mouth.

He pushed open a door, leading her into a dark bedroom. She saw a window on the wall, a bit of light seeping in from the streetlight outside. He was behind her suddenly, grabbing hold of her zipper.

"What are you doing?" she asked, though she couldn't move.

"Just hold still," he whispered, his words dripping with disdain.

"Alex, please don't," she pleaded, her body beginning to tremble. His lips were on her skin, his hands pulling her dress down over her hips. She went rigid as he pressed his body onto hers, his arms around her waist. "Alex," she said again. "I don't want this."

Suddenly, she heard someone moving on the other side of the room, a belt buckle jingling. "Who's there?" she asked, cool tears filling her eyes.

The light to the room flicked on and the blurry image in front of her took shape.

"Gunner?" She heaved a sigh of relief at seeing a familiar face. He stood in front of her, his face twisted in anger. He was shirtless, buttoning and adjusting his pants. Beside him, stood a girl she vaguely knew from school, Dana Hively—her long black hair dancing carelessly over her bare breasts. She grabbed a shirt off the bed upon seeing them and attempted to cover herself. "What are you doing, baby?" she asked him, kissing his cheek and trying to pull him back to the bed.

"Get out of here," he told the girl, who disappeared out the

door in nothing but an oversized t-shirt, a frustrated look on her face.

Behind her, Alex had frozen, though she still stood exposed to them both. Snapping into action, she pulled her dress back up, her eyes continuing to fill with silent tears. Gunner approached her, his eyes locked with Alex's. "Go, Reagan," he told her.

Reagan nodded, taking a step forward. Alex grabbed hold of her arm. "I don't think so. This isn't your concern. We're just having some fun."

Like lightning, Gunner reached across, ripping Alex's hand off Reagan. "The fun is over," he said firmly.

"What's your problem, man?"

"My problem is you. What would Mommy and Daddy think if they just happened to hear their precious baby boy is forcing himself onto drunk girls at parties?"

"You're full of shit,"Alex said, looking Gunner square in the eye.

"Try me," Gunner dared him, taking a step closer. His shoulder brushed Reagan's as he neared her attacker.

"Whatever, dude," Alex said angrily, taking a step back. "It ain't worth it for some drunk slut. You can have her." He laughed casually, though his voice still radiated anger, and sauntered in between them, nearly shoving Reagan down. She took a half-step to keep herself from falling.

"See you around, Reagan," he purred her name, giving her one last look before he disappeared out the door.

Gunner was at her side in an instant, scooping her up in his arms with ease. He walked her across the room, setting her down on the bed and brushing her hair back off her shoulders.

"You okay?" he asked.

She nodded, though she wasn't sure how true that was.

"He won't bother you again," he said firmly. And somehow, she believed him.

"He's just a dumb guy, Gunner," she said softly. "Showing off 'cause I turned his friend down. Getting even." Her voice was bitter as she remembered his hands on her, his rough touch.

"Don't justify what he did," he said defensively. "Don't you dare."

She laid back on the bed, her entire world spinning. He eased down beside her cautiously, their heads side by side. He turned to look at her.

"I'm fine now," she said, staring straight ahead. "You can go back to your date."

"She wasn't my date."

"No? It certainly looked like it."

"Trust me, she wasn't a date. Dana Hively doesn't date."

"Oh, but Gunner James does?" she asked, looking at him then. Their faces were only a few inches apart, noses practically touching.

"Who's asking?"

"Someone who has heard the rumors." She spoke without reservation thanks to the alcohol in her stomach.

"And what rumors would that be?" he asked, his eyes dancing between hers.

"Oh, please Gunner. You don't date. You are too cool for that. Or, at least, you think you are."

"Says who?"

"People."

"People don't know me," he said adamantly, lifting himself up and propping his head into his palm.

"Some people know you."

"Like who?" he asked. "You?"

She shook her head, her lips pressed together. "I know of you, Gunner. I don't know you."

"You don't want to know me, princess."

She covered her face, groaning. "Oh, here we go again."

"I saved your ass tonight. I reserve the right to call you princess." He half-laughed.

Her face grew serious as she stared at him. "Yeah," she said finally. "Yeah, you did. You saved me tonight. Just like you saved me before."

"Yeah, so remember that next time you want to give me lip," he said, brushing his finger over her bottom lip so it made a popping noise when it bounced back to the top.

"Why are you always saving me, Gunner James?" she asked, not laughing at his joke.

He shrugged his shoulders, breaking eye contact. "It's not a big deal. I've just been in the right place at the right time."

"No," she said, sitting up so that she was level with him. The room was suddenly eerily still. She placed a hand on his cheek for a second but moved it away. "No matter how you try to justify it, you've saved me. Cleaned up the messes I managed to get myself into."

"It's not a big—"

"Thank you," she said firmly.

He stopped talking, his jaw tight, eyes avoiding hers. "You're welcome," he said, obviously feeling the tension in the room.

She laid back down, waiting until he did the same before she spoke again. "Do you go around saving all the princesses?" she asked, elbowing him playfully.

"Nah, just my favorites." She spied the smile that grew on his face, though he was staring at the ceiling.

"You're my favorite knight," she said, smiling back.

"I'm more like a villain." His gaze fell to her.

"Villains don't save princesses," she said. "Haven't you ever read a fairytale?"

He laughed. "Not lately."

She rolled over to face him, her body pressing into his side. "Well, knights save princesses, for your information."

"I'll remember that for when I'm on Jeopardy."

"Or princes," she said. "Remember that too."

"I'll remember."

She rested her head on his chest, listening to his heartbeat as it picked up speed. "Will you remember me?" she asked, her voice vulnerable.

"Huh?"

"When you're off with whatever girl you hook up with at the next party...will you remember me? Remember this? You could be this guy if you wanted, Gunner. You could be a prince."

He sat up, holding her shoulders firmly. "We should get you home," he said.

"What? Why?" she asked, her face growing warm with embarrassment. She'd let the liquor start talking too much.

"Because it's late and I'm heading home and there's no way in hell I'm leaving you here alone."

"See," she said, as he grabbed hold of her hand and pulled her out of the room. "You're always saving me."

He ignored her comment, pulling her through the crowds of people. She ignored everyone around, her eyes locked only on him. She should have found Emily, let her know she was leaving, but rational thought had all gone out the window.

He led her to his car, starting it up without a word. He pointed to the glove box. "There's some eye drops in there. If your parents will still be awake, you'll want to use them so your eyes aren't so red. Get some gum, too, so the liquor smell won't be so strong. You can roll down your window to help you sober up a bit, if you want," he instructed her.

"What about my clothes? I reek. He spilled a drink on me."

"I'm not exactly your size," he said, "so I can't help you there."

"Gunner James is out of options?" she teased, grabbing a bottle of cologne out of his floorboard and spraying it onto herself.

"You're going to smell like me now," he said worriedly.

"Is that a bad thing?" she asked. And it wasn't. The cologne had a nice scent, though it wasn't one she recognized. She ran her fingers over the glass skull on the lid.

He pulled up to her house, putting the car in park just as the front porch light flicked on. "Here's your stop."

"Did you want to walk me to the door?" she asked softly, hoping.

"That's not a good idea." He shook his head. He wasn't looking at her.

"Why not?"

He turned to her, staring her down. "Because, Reagan." It shocked her to hear him using her name. She liked the way it sounded rolling off his tongue. "I told you...I'm a villain. And villains don't get the princess."

SEVEN

GUNNER
PRESENT DAY

Gunner was roused from sleep by a knock on his door. He rolled over, sitting up in bed. "Come in," he called, still half asleep. The door cracked open and his mother peered in.

"Good morning," she said.

"Good morning."

"You got in after I was already asleep last night. I didn't get to ask you how it went."

"It went fine," he said, rubbing his eyes and yawning.

"I can't imagine that's true," she said, her arms crossed in front of her.

"Yeah," he said simply, "I guess you're right."

"How did they take the news?"

"They already knew. I didn't have to break it to them."

She shook her head. "Bless their hearts. I'll make them some food for you to take by later."

"I really don't think that's a good idea, Mom."

"Why not?"

"I don't want to bother them."

She sighed, sitting down beside him on the bed. She moved a piece of hair from his eyes carefully. "Okay, Gunner, getting straight to the point. Did you see Reagan last night? Or are you planning to avoid her?"

"I'm not planning to avoid anyone, but I don't intend to see her any more than I have to. I'm here for Holly's funeral. I owe her that much."

"Because she was Reagan's sister."

"Because she was a friend. I want to pay my respects."

"Gunner—"

"Mom," he said firmly, cutting her off before softening his tone. "I'm sorry, it's not your fault. I just really don't want to talk about it."

"Fine," she said, "but you will go over and drop off the casserole I'm going to make. I don't care what's going on between you and that girl—you aren't going to be rude to her grieving family."

"Why do you care? You never cared about our relationship before," he argued.

"You know that's not true."

He shrugged.

"Either way, you're going to take that casserole over. You two need to talk. No more arguing."

"Okay, fine," he agreed begrudgingly.

"So," she said, her eyebrows raised. "Did you meet anyone new last night?"

"New? Like who?"

"Like...Nora?"

"Nora?" he asked.

His mother's face grew worried. "It was late when you got there. She was probably already in bed. I just assumed she might've...told you," she rambled on, not making any sense to him.

"Hang on a second, who's Nora?"

"You should probably ask Reagan yourself."

"Mom," he demanded, "who's Nora?"

She sighed heavily, patting his hand. "Nora is Reagan's daughter, Gunner." She paused, letting it sink in. "And, I'm assuming she's yours, too."

EIGHT

GUNNER

Gunner stood in front of the door, his heart pounding once again. He pressed his finger into the doorbell, one he'd pressed so many times before. Gemma answered the door after a few moments, still in her nightgown. Her eyes were red and swollen, fresh tears lining them. She looked as though she hadn't slept a wink.

"Gunner?" she asked, confusion filling her face.

He held out the casserole. "My mom wanted me to bring this over. She said to let her know if there's anything at all she can do."

"Well, that was very kind of her," she said, shock in her voice. "Your mother's Misty, right? Misty Hodges? I think she and Scott were the same grade in school. For such a small town, it always shocks me the people I haven't met. You think you know everyone." She shrugged, wiping away a tear.

"Yes, Hodges then. James now," he informed her. "She doesn't get out much."

"Right." She nodded. "Well, that's too bad. Anyway, tell her thank you from us. This is kind of her." She took the dish from his hands carefully.

Shifting in place, he frowned. "I'll pass on the message."

When he didn't turn to leave, Gemma set the casserole down on a nearby table and stepped back. "Would you like to come in?"

"Actually, I was hoping to see Reagan," he said sheepishly, not moving.

"She's not here, Gunner. She's at home."

"Home?"

"She's twenty six years old. Surely you didn't expect her to still be living here?" she said, her tone slow and understanding rather than harsh.

He shook his head. "I guess you're right. It's strange to think of her living anywhere else."

"A lot has changed since you left. I'll tell her you stopped by," she said, moving to shut the door.

He put his hand out, catching the wood. "Actually, I was hoping you could tell me where she lives."

She looked as though she were thinking about his request for a moment before shaking her head. "I don't think that would be such a good idea, Gunner."

"Please," he begged, feeling uncomfortably exposed. Gunner James didn't ask for things, didn't need help from anyone.

She looked to the ground. "You broke her heart," she said simply. "You just...left. Her father and I watched her cry for weeks on end, waiting for you to come back."

"I'm sorry, Gemma—"

"I don't know what happened between the two of you. And frankly, it's none of my business, but Reagan has worked hard to get where she's at now. Happy. She has a good life, Gunner. Please, *please* don't take that away from her."

"I'm sorry," he said again, hoping she believed how much he meant it. It had been a mistake to come there. He backed away in retreat, his head down. "I won't be bothering you again."

As he made his way down the short sidewalk toward his car, he heard her voice. "The old Cameron house." He turned back around, his head cocked. "My parents left it to her when they died."

He nodded, feeling hope fill him. "Thank you," he called to her, bowing his head.

"You didn't hear it from me." She stared at him firmly. It was a warning.

"Hear what?" He grinned, climbing into his car and pulling away.

NINE

REAGAN

December 2008

Reagan opened her locker, the familiar red envelope fluttering to the floor and causing her heart to skip a beat. She bent down, picking up the invitation and unsealing it, her pulse racing. On the inside, she'd written a simple note: ***Go to prom with me?*** *Over the question, he'd written his answer in thick, black marker. A single word:* ***No.***

Her heart sank. She crushed the letter, tossing it and the envelope into the nearest garbage can and darted down the hallway. She pushed open the door, moving in between the crowd of students on her way to her car. She was unlocking it when she caught a glimpse of him, walking slowly toward his own car, seemingly lost in thought.

She raced up to him. "Who the hell do you think you are saying no to me?" she half-joked.

He blinked out of his trance, a confident grin on his face. "I'm Gunner James, haven't we met?"

"Gunner, go to prom with me," she propositioned him again.

"No fucking way." He shook his head, resting a hand on the hood of his car as they reached it.

"Why not?" she demanded indignantly.

He looked down at himself, holding his hands up. "What about me screams 'cheap suits and flowers' to you?"

"You go to parties all the time."

"Parties aren't prom, Reagan."

"So, you honestly won't go with me?"

He held up two fingers. "Scout's honor."

She huffed, crossing her arms. "Well, what would you rather us do that night then?"

"What?"

"If we skip prom, what are we doing instead?"

"Who's we?"

"Me and you."

"Reagan, no." He lowered his brow, speaking slowly as if she were a child. "There is no 'me and you'."

"Yes, I know. You've told me."

"Because—"

"Because I'm a princess and you're not," she repeated his words, her eyes rolling.

"Not even in the prettiest dress and crown." A smile spread across his lips.

"So, I'm converting," she said plainly.

"Do what?"

"I'm converting. To...villain, or whatever. I'm whatever you are."

He sighed. "Not possible."

"You're being difficult."

"I'm being realistic."

"Don't you like me?" she asked, adrenaline coursing through her.

Seemingly caught off-guard, he stammered. "That—that's not the point."

"So, you do, then. And I like you," she told him boldly.

He pressed his lips together. "You don't know me."

"And you don't know me. But we can fix that pretty easily," she said in a sing-song voice.

"It's not going to work, Reagan, okay?" he said, his words sharp. His tone stung her as she realized she wasn't going to win.

"Fine," she said sternly, crossing her arms and storming away. She listened carefully, waiting for him to call out to her, but he didn't. Instead, she heard his car rev up and his tires screech and she knew he was gone.

TEN

REAGAN

December 2008

The next week after school, Reagan caught up with Holly, surprised to see her walking with a familiar face.

"Holly!" she called.

Her sister turned around to face her. "Yeah?" she asked.

"What are you doing? Do you two need a ride? You're Gia, right?" she introduced herself to the girl. "Reagan."

"Yeah, I know who you are," the girl said shyly. "I usually just walk. I'll catch up with you later, Holly." She waved at them both, turning to walk the opposite direction.

"What was that about?" Holly asked her once Gia was out of earshot.

"That was Gia James, right?"

"Yeah, why?"

"Are you two friends? I've never seen you with her."

"We're working together on a project for chemistry.

What's going on with you? Why the sudden interest in my social life?"

"No reason," Reagan lied. "I'm friends with her brother."

Holly's jaw dropped. "Gavin? Since when? He's seriously hot."

"No," Reagan said, waving her arm. "Not freaky twin brother. I'm friends with Gunner."

Holly crinkled her nose as if she'd smelled something bad. "Oh, ew."

"Don't be like that," Reagan snapped defensively.

"I could understand Gavin—like I said, hot. But Gunner is...creepy. And bad news."

"He is not," she said firmly. "He's really sweet."

Holly shook her head. "There is nothing about that boy that says sweet. He looks like he needs a shower. And I know he needs a truancy officer. And probably an STD test."

"You're being dramatic, you just don't know him like I do," Reagan told her.

Holly shrugged. "Whatever you say. Just be careful. That family is seriously messed up."

"Meaning what?" Reagan sensed the dark tone in her voice.

She shook her head, glancing at her quickly and then back down. She spoke softly, though no one was around. "I don't know anything for sure."

"But you suspect?"

"Gia comes to school with bruises. A lot of bruises. Gavin sometimes, too."

Reagan gasped. "Oh, no." She covered her mouth in disbelief.

"Like I said, I have no way of knowing for sure."

"We have to tell someone, Holly," Reagan said, a sick feeling washing over her.

"I'm not getting involved. Gia hasn't told me anything herself and Gavin is a big guy. I'm sure he can take care of himself. I only told you so you'd be careful. I don't know what Gunner could be capable of."

"He'd never hurt me." She dismissed the idea quickly.

"Whatever you say. I'm just warning you...be careful."

"Okay," Reagan said. "Well, thanks. I will."

Holly nodded. "Now, are you still offering me a ride?"

"Sure," Reagan agreed, lost in her own troubled thoughts.

ELEVEN

REAGAN

January 2009

Reagan sat in her bedroom, listening to her stereo. Okay, in truth, her music was turned down so low she could hardly hear it. Instead, she was trying desperately to listen to the muffled voices in the next room. She pressed her ear to the wall she shared with Holly.

They were laughing, their voices low. What on Earth could they be talking about? She knew Holly must be in heaven, both Gia and Gavin had been in her room for over an hour and Holly's high-pitched flirting laugh had been on full display for at least half of that.

Suddenly her door opened, causing her to jump. Gunner stood in her doorway, his face as red as she felt her own becoming.

"Oh, shit. Sorry," he said, covering his mouth.

"What are you doing here?" she asked, increasingly aware that he was in her bedroom.

"I'm here to pick up my brother and sister. Your mom said second door on the right." He looked back out into the hall, counting.

"She must not have been counting the linen closet. Holly's room is the next one."

"Oh, okay," he said, beginning to leave.

"Gunner, wait!" she called out to him.

He stopped. "Yeah?"

She looked him over, trying to spot any bruises he might have. It had been a while since she'd seen him and Holly's words were still fresh on her mind. To her relief, she didn't find any. "I, um, I got you something." She hopped off the bed, walking to her closet. She dug to the back, pulling out a hanger and revealing the tuxedo her father had helped her pick out.

He stared at it, his face firm. "What's that?"

"It's, um, well...my dad said you could have it. Borrow it. Whatever. It's yours if you want it. We guessed at your size." She stared at the tux, her body shaking with nervousness.

He shut the door. "Do you think I can't afford to buy my own?" he asked, his tone defensive.

"I didn't want that to be the reason we didn't go."

"I work two jobs, Reagan. I don't need your family's money."

"Fine then," she said, laying the hanger on the bed. "You don't have to take it. It was just an offer."

"What did you tell your father?"

"What do you mean?"

"About why you were buying that for me."

She lowered her eyebrows in confusion. "I asked him if we could get you one when we went shopping for my dress."

"But why? I mean, you obviously didn't tell him you were planning to go with me." He scoffed. His voice was hard and tough, though his eyes had a hint of vulnerability.

"Of course I did. Why wouldn't I?" she asked, crossing her arms.

"Because...because I'm me," he said, as if that were enough explanation.

"What's wrong with being you?" She took a step toward him.

"You mean your parents are actually okay with you going to prom with the town screw-up?" He laughed cautiously.

"Gunner...I don't think of you that way. You shouldn't talk like that."

"And why not? We both know my family is a smudge on this town's map."

"I don't care what your family is. I care about you."

He shook his head. "Your father is the president of a bank, Reagan. Mine is the president of a bar stool at Richie's. We come from different worlds."

She grimaced. "I am not my family." She took another step toward him, placing a careful hand on his chest. He didn't move away, his eyes locked on hers. "And you are not yours."

"You don't know what you're saying."

"You said you liked me."

"It doesn't matter how I feel, Reagan."

"It matters to me."

"I just...I can't. We can't." He stepped back, causing her hand to fall from his chest.

"Why?" she demanded. "I want to know why."

"You're...you. You're Reagan Orrick. Untouchable. You need to be with someone who is...like you."

She pulled his hand to her face, his skin burning hers. "I am not untouchable. And I am not looking for anyone like me. I want you, Gunner. Why can't you just accept that?"

His expression warmed slightly, a small smile on his lips. His thumb caressed her cheekbone. "You aren't used to being told no, are you?"

"Nope," she told him honestly.

He shook his head. "I'm not making any promises to be who you want me to be."

"You already are."

His eyes grew dark. "I'm serious, Reagan. You think you know me because you've seen me in a few of my better moments, but that doesn't make me good. You don't know the real me. And I won't apologize for who I am."

She leaned forward on a whim and pressed her lips to his cheek. He froze, his body rigid. When she pulled away, she locked her eyes with his once more. "I don't want you to be anyone else. I want to know you."

He was silent for a moment, thinking. Finally, he spoke. "I won't wear that tux. I don't need a handout. I can buy one for myself."

"You'll go?" she squealed, clasping her hands in front of her chest. Her smile grew wide.

He sighed. "One night. It's not a promise of anything else. Just one night, Reagan. Don't go getting any ideas about us."

She leapt up, throwing her arms around his neck. He didn't kiss her, though she desperately wanted him to. Instead, he touched her shoulder gently, a small worried smile on his face. He brushed a piece of hair from her eyes and stepped back. "Well, I should be going."

"You don't have to."

"I have to get Gavin and Gia home. Mom will be worrying."

"Okay," she said softly, feeling disappointed. He began to leave the room but stopped. Hope filled her for just a moment. "What color is your dress?"

She paused. "Red. Why?"

"I have to match, right? Those flowery things? A tie?"

"Right. Do you want me to go with you?"

"Yeah, okay."

"Really?" She was taken by surprise at his quick answer.

"Yeah."

"This weekend?"

"I'll see what I can do," he said casually.

"You aren't just saying that, right? I don't need you to lie to me just to get me to shut up. Don't blow me off, Gunner."

He opened the door, stepping out into the hallway without a glance back her way. "I'll see you tomorrow."

TWELVE

GUNNER
PRESENT DAY

Gunner pulled up to the old Cameron house less than half an hour later. Reagan had painted the old wood siding a bright yellow and the once black shutters were now baby blue. He smiled slightly, the sunshine she so effortlessly brought into every aspect of her life shone from the corner lot of this drab neighborhood. A large flower garden lit up the front yard.

He walked up the paved path to the front door cautiously, his pulse racing. Everything in him screamed that he should turn around, but his feet kept moving. He had to know the truth. As he reached the wooden, white door and rapped his knuckles on it, he cleared his throat, waiting.

The door opened almost immediately and Reagan stood in front of him. Her blonde hair had been thrown up into a disheveled ponytail, she wore a blue robe, and her eyes were swollen and red—further proof of her suffering.

She didn't look surprised to see him and he wondered if Gemma had called to warn her. "What do you want, Gunner?"

"I know I'm the last person you want to see right now."

She snorted. "You think?"

"But we need to talk."

"We have nothing to talk about. You're eight years too late for that." She crossed her arms over her chest, the pain evident on her face.

"Am I?" he asked, then when she didn't answer, he went on. "You deserve answers."

"That's an understatement." She pressed her lips together, unmoving.

"But, I deserve answers too, Reagan." She flinched slightly as he said her name, her eyes faltering for just a second.

"What's that supposed to mean? I'm not the one who just...just disappeared out of nowhere."

"You aren't innocent here. Not completely."

"What the hell are you saying, Gunner?"

"I know about Nora."

She stepped toward him, shock filling her eyes. Her body filled the gap in between the door and its frame, making it impossible for him to see into the house. "Don't you dare talk about her."

He held his hands up, hearing the tears in her shaking voice. "I don't want to upset you, Rae. That's not my intention. I just want to talk."

"I don't want to talk to you. Eight years ago, seven,

maybe even six...I *dreamed* that we'd be having this conversation. I dreamed you'd come here...that you'd come home to me. But not now. Not like this. I quit waiting for you a long time ago. And frankly, you being home is the last thing I need right now."

"I know this is a bad time. Hell, that's an understatement, too. I didn't come back to complicate things for you. I wanted you to know I'm...I'm really sorry about Holly. She was a good kid."

"You didn't know her," she snapped.

"Not like I know you, no, but enough. Enough to be sorry she's gone. And to be sorry you're hurting."

"You don't know me, Gunner. I'm not the same little girl you used to know. And you never cared about my pain before, sure as hell not when you were the one causing it. Why start now?" she snarled at him, her voice rising in anger.

"What? Like you never hurt me?" He stopped himself before he said too much. This wasn't what he wanted and it wasn't going to get them anywhere.

"Screw you. Why don't you just go back to wherever the hell you came from? You don't belong here anymore. I don't want you here."

He put his hand up to stop her as she moved to shut the door. "Wait. I'm sorry, okay? I didn't come here to fight with you."

"Why did you come here, then?"

"I wanted to see you," he said honestly.

"Well, I don't want to see you."

He sighed. "Can you at least tell me about Nora?"

"She's with her grandparents."

"That's not what I meant."

"You didn't want to hear about her before."

"That's not true," he argued. "You didn't even try—"

"You were gone," she said through gritted teeth. "I tried to find you but you were just...gone. What was I supposed to do?"

"I didn't have a choice."

"There's always a choice, Gunner. But, the thing is, I don't care about your reasons anymore. I don't. So, you can save whatever excuse you have. I don't want to hear it."

"You owe me the truth about her," he said, "no matter what your feelings are for me."

"What? What truth do you want? Are you asking if she's yours?" she asked, her face firm.

"Yes," he confirmed. "Is she mine? Or is she his?"

THIRTEEN

REAGAN

March 2009

When prom night finally arrived, Reagan stood in her living room, watching out the window for him to arrive. Holly walked past her, dressed in a pair of flannel pajamas that belonged to Reagan, but she was too excited to scold her.

"Lover boy here yet?" her father asked, walking into the room with a mug of coffee in his hand.

She groaned. "Dad, please don't be embarrassing."

"Oh, no. Please do." Holly plopped on the couch as if this were to be her evening entertainment.

"I'll try my best," Scott joked, patting Reagan's hair.

Reagan smoothed it over immediately, rushing to a mirror to make sure it wasn't out of place. She heard his car, her heart lurching with excitement as she rushed to the window and peered out of the blinds. Confirming her hopes, she saw the headlights coming down her street. The car stopped in front of her house. She shut the blinds hurriedly, backing away as she heard his engine shut off and the car door being slammed shut.

She paced in front of the door, her heart pounding, waiting for his knock. When it finally came, she counted to three silently so as not to seem overly anxious before opening it. She took a deep breath, looking him over. He stood in the threshold; a thin, black suit hung loosely over his frame. It needed to be tailored, but she wouldn't dare mention it. A red tie was wrapped around his neck, the knot messy and unflattering, but still, she couldn't take her eyes off of him. In the dark suit, his chestnut eyes seemed even more mysterious. He'd gotten a haircut to surprise her, his thick, black hair now several inches shorter than it had been. He'd slicked the top part back, reminding her of a hairstyle from the fifties.

Still staring at him, she realized in a breath how truly gorgeous he was. Tall, dark, and handsome, he literally took her breath away. Finally, he cleared his throat, interrupting her thoughts. He reached a hand out past her to shake her father's.

"Mr. Orrick."

"Gunner," her father greeted him warmly. Her mother rushed into the room, camera in hand.

"Oh, you two look so beautiful," she gushed, tears in her eyes.

"Gemma—" Scott warned, smiling dotingly at his wife.

She wiped a tear away. "My baby girl is going to prom. I'm allowed to be emotional," she teased. "Did I miss the corsage?"

Reagan panicked. Gunner hadn't been able to buy her a corsage when they'd gone shopping for the tie. He claimed it was because he wanted to surprise her, but she'd seen him counting the money in his wallet when he thought she wasn't paying attention.

"Oh, mom. I don't need a—"

He cut her off by reaching into the inside pocket of his jacket and pulling out a small white box. He held it out to her, a red flower sitting on top of a lace band. "Do you like it?" he asked, hope in his eyes. She could tell it mattered to him.

"It's perfect," she said, completely caught off guard. She allowed him to slide the corsage over her wrist as her mother snapped a few pictures.

"All right, now get together," Gemma instructed, taking a few more. Reagan hardly noticed her parents. Her heart was beating a mile a minute, her face on fire as he slid his arm around her waist to pose for the last picture.

Beside her, Holly held out the white faux fur jacket she'd laid on the couch earlier. Reagan took it, throwing it over her shoulders carefully.

"Thanks," she said, smiling at her sister.

"Now, you guys be careful," her father warned. "And don't stay out too late."

"And have fun," her mother called, waving to them as they walked out the front door.

Gunner visibly relaxed as they exited the house. He took her hand, lacing his fingers with hers. "You look nice," he told her.

"So do you," she said honestly.

When they got to the car, he opened her door for her, picking up the back of her dress and helping her place it into the car with care. She smiled at him happily.

"Thank you."

He walked around the car, climbing into the driver's seat and starting it up. "Last chance to change your mind," he teased, glancing at her with a sly smile.

She shook her head defiantly. "Not a chance, Mr. James." She slid her hand back into his. His skin was warm on hers, his palms rough. He held her hand tight, not bothering to pull away until they drove into the school parking lot. The small lot was lined with limousines, their classmates flooding out of them.

He pulled the car into the far corner and stuffed a pack of cigarettes into the inside pocket of his jacket before getting out.

"What, no flask?" she joked. His eyes went dark, his face stern and she realized her mistake instantly. The joke wasn't funny to the son of the town drunk.

"No," he said after a moment, "no flask."

She wanted to apologize but worried it would only make things more awkward, so she remained silent as he walked around to help her out of the car. She ignored the strange looks she got as they walked into the school. People were surprised to see her with him. She had expected it, though it didn't make it any easier or less annoying.

She put her arm through his, trying to show him how little she cared about the opinions of others. She knew what the issue was—the one they all, Gunner included, seemed to be fixated on: they weren't alike. She was light where Gunner was dark; the bad boy and the princess. They couldn't be more opposite and yet she had never felt more comfortable than there in his arms. Rules and opinions be damned, she was falling for Gunner, and if she had her way...she'd make sure he fell for her, too.

They walked into the gymnasium, the room illuminated by pink lanterns. She stared around, several eyes on them. Quickly, Gunner pulled her into a dark corner.

"What are you doing?" she asked.

"Wait here. I'll go get us something to drink."

She nodded, taking a seat on the bleachers to wait for him. He was gone only a moment or two, and when he returned, he held two clear cups in his hands. She took one graciously, downing the punch in two gulps. She hadn't realized how dry her throat had been until that moment.

Gunner pulled his cup from his lips, sitting down beside her and smiling. "Do you need more?" He offered his up. It was the most intimate she'd ever felt: sitting in the dark gymnasium, sharing a glass of tasteless punch. She took a sip from the cup, handing it back. He drank the rest, crushing the clear plastic easily and tossing it into a nearby garbage can.

"I'm glad we came," she told him.

He leaned forward to face her, brushing a stray piece of hair from her eyes. "Don't say that until the night's over."

She silenced him by leaning her head onto his shoulder. "I'm serious," she assured him. "I'm glad we're here. Thank you for agreeing to come with me."

He surprised her by laying his head over onto hers. "Do you want to dance?" She heard the question, though she was in utter shock.

She pulled back, looking up at him. "Seriously?" She looked at the empty dance floor with apprehension. "You'll dance with me?"

He smirked, running a hand through his hair. "I mean, look, I'm not promising a waltz or anything, but I can stand awkwardly and move in a circle with the best of 'em."

She stared at the boy who was still such a mystery to her in awe. "I'd like that a lot."

Without another word, he stood up, taking her hand in his and pulling her to the dance floor. She followed him dreamily, forgetting about everyone else in the room. He stopped in the middle of the gym floor, his eyes locked on hers as he placed his hands around her waist carefully. Unlike the dance partners—though limited—she'd had before, Gunner didn't stare off awkwardly, avoiding her eye contact. Instead, his gaze stayed focused on her confidently as they began to sway.

She smiled at him. "Regretting your decision yet?"

He shook his head. "Worrying you'll be regretting yours soon."

"You really think I'd rather be here with," she paused, glancing around and nodding her head in the general direction of a group of jocks, "one of them?"

He looked their way and then back at her. "I think you're supposed to be here with one of them."

"When are you going to realize I couldn't care less what I'm supposed to do?"

He sighed, his face wavering as he stared at her. His eyes darted back and forth between hers. Kiss me, *she begged silently.*

"Have you guys gotten a chance to vote for prom King and Queen yet?" a small voice asked from behind her. Reagan turned around, ending their dance. Dana Hively held up a small clipboard, a giant smile on her face. "Wow," she said, ignoring Reagan. "Gunner, you look great." She looked him up and down as if he were a piece of meat.

He held out his hand for the clipboard. "Don't worry,

Dana. You know I'm voting for you," he said, laughter in his voice. "You don't have to flatter me."

"I would really appreciate it," she said, pretending to be shocked.

Suddenly, Reagan remembered the night at the party when she'd caught Dana and Gunner in the bedroom together and her belly filled with unsubstantiated jealousy. He held out the clipboard for Reagan to vote, and she did so begrudgingly. She handed the ballot back, her hands shaking, and waited for the girl to walk away.

Once she was gone, she turned back to face Gunner, her arms around his neck once more. She tried to push the anger from her mind.

"You weren't on the ballot?" she asked.

"Are you surprised?"

She shook her head.

"I wasn't planning on being here tonight. I spend all my time avoiding this place, remember?"

She laughed half-heartedly. "How could I forget?"

"What's wrong?" he asked, reading her expression.

"Nothing."

"Yeah, right. Did I do something?"

"No," she assured him. "I just...it's stupid. I recognized her from that night. The party. You two were..." She trailed off, unable to say it. The image had been burned into her mind. "I know I have no right to be...whatever I am, but it caught me by surprise."

His worry changed to a cocky grin instantly. "You're jealous?"

"Don't tease," she warned.

"I never thought I'd see the day."

"What day?"

"The day that Reagan Orrick was jealous of anyone."

"Don't do that." She narrowed her eyes at him.

"Do what?"

"Don't say my name like that. Like it's a title or something. Of course I'm jealous. Because she's gorgeous and you've slept with her. And I had to witness it."

He rubbed a finger over her cheek. "You're gorgeous, Rae. You don't have to worry about Dana. Besides, I'm sure there are a few guys in this room I should be jealous of."

She bit her lip, shaking her head slightly. His eyes grew wide as the song changed to something more upbeat. Around them, the floor began to fill with people, yet they stood still, staring at each other in shock. After a moment of processing, he pulled her off the dance floor, back to the solace of their corner.

"No?" he asked over the music.

"No," she said.

"No one here?"

"No one period." She blushed.

"Holy shit." He ran a hand over his jaw, looking away from her. He shook his head. "Please tell me you're not saying what I think you're saying."

"Are you asking?"

He looked back, his stare burning into her as his expression changed slightly. "You aren't serious."

"Of course I am. I mean, I've done...things, just not everything." She suddenly felt embarrassed by the virtue she'd always taken such pride in.

"Okay," he said simply, shoving a hand into his pocket. "I need to go outside for a minute and get some air. Do you want

to come with me or stay here?" His facial muscles were strangely tight.

She glanced around. "I don't think we're allowed to leave." She pointed to the chaperoned doors.

He smirked. "You underestimate me, princess."

She took his outstretched hand without thought. "Lead the way."

He led her through the boy's locker room and into a dark, janitor's closet she hadn't known about. There was a door leading to the parking lot. The handle was labeled: EMERGENCY ONLY: ALARM WILL SOUND. *Gunner pushed the door open without hesitation and to Reagan's relief no alarms began blaring.*

He walked to the side of the building and leaned up against it, pulling out a cigarette. He lit it, inhaling deeply, the smoke dancing as it exited his lips. She watched in amusement.

"Everything okay?" he asked her, noticing her stares.

"Why do you smoke?"

"Does it bother you?" He flicked ash from the end.

"It's just a question," she said softly.

"I don't know. Just to pass the time, I guess."

"Do your parents know?" It was rare that she brought up his parents, but she was genuinely curious.

"You gonna tell 'em?" he asked, taking another puff and throwing the butt down. He smashed it with his foot.

"My parents would kill me," she told him. "Holly got caught with one last year. One. It was like World War III for days."

"My parents don't care." He shrugged.

"They don't care that you smoke?"

"They don't care about much." He didn't bother to elaborate.

"I'd like to meet them," she said, though she was unsure if that were true.

"No," he said quickly. "That won't happen."

"Well, not right now. Not tonight." She laughed. "But eventually, right?"

"No, Reagan." His voice was serious.

She didn't know what to say, though she was growing increasingly upset by his harshness. "You don't think they'll like me?"

"Trust me, that's not it." He touched her hand, his tone softening.

"Then, what is it?"

"What's with the third degree?" he asked, pulling his hand back. "Let's just go back in." He started to walk away, but she grabbed his shoulders, pushing his back onto the brick of the school. In the heels she had on, she was practically his height.

"Woah, easy tiger." He winked.

"I want to know you, Gunner."

"What?" He furrowed his brow.

"You said I don't know you. You said I only know one side of you. I want to change that. I want to know more about you."

"There's nothing to tell."

"Cut the crap," she told him pointedly.

"Feisty, aren't you?" He tried to turn the conversation playful, but she wasn't having it.

"I want past this wall you have up. I told you something

really personal about myself earlier, something I don't just go around announcing. Now, it's your turn."

He stared, his eyes darting in between hers. Finally, he nodded. "You really want to know me?" he asked, taking off his jacket.

"Yes."

"Fine. First things first, let's get the hell out of here."

THEY SAT *in his car at Smoot Park, finishing off the last bit of their fast food. "So this is what you do in your spare time?" she asked, popping a fry in her mouth.*

"Among other things."

"Like?"

"Like...well, I play guitar."

"Of course you do."

"And...I like to read."

"You read?" she asked, unable to hide her shock.

"Uh, yeah, I did finish first grade," he said sarcastically at her wide-eyed expression.

"But...I've never seen you read. You hate school."

"I don't have time for school. There's a difference. It's not about hate. I work two jobs and spend the rest of my time trying to stay out of my dad's way. Forgive me if the Pythagorean Theorem isn't on the top of my to-do list."

"Stay out of your dad's way? Is he mean?" she asked boldly, unsure if it was okay to bring up.

"He's an old drunk," Gunner said firmly. "They traditionally aren't who you want to have around at family dinner." They were both silent for a moment before he went

on. "He's not as bad to me as he is the rest of my family. That's why I try to keep them safe."

"You can't put that on yourself. You're still just a kid, Gunner."

"I haven't been able to be a kid for a long time."

"That's not fair to you. You can be a kid with me. Sometimes you just need that."

"I don't want to be a kid with you, Reagan. I really, really want to be a man with you." His voice grew heated, causing her insides to twist as she wondered if he meant what she thought he did. "And that, unfortunately, is one of the many reasons why we will never work like you want us to. Because, at the end of the day, you are still very much a kid and I...well, I have never really been one."

"I'm less than a year younger than you," she argued.

"It really has nothing to do with age."

"Just because I'm a virgin doesn't mean I'm innocent."

"This goes so much deeper than that," he said, twisting his hands on the steering wheel. "It's not about sex. It's about the darkness I've seen, the things I've experienced...things I never, ever want you to have to know about." He dropped his hands from the steering wheel, turning to face her and taking her hand in his. "I like that you're a light in my all-too-dark world, but it's selfish of me to bring you into my darkness. You deserve to keep seeing the world like you do. And to be with me, to really truly be with me, would be to take some of that light away from you. I don't think I could forgive myself for that."

"You talk about me like I'm so perfect, but I'm not. And, no, my life may not have been as dark as yours, but that doesn't mean I haven't hurt. You don't get to monopolize

pain, Gunner. And no matter how many times you try to tell me why we won't work, I'm going to keep telling you why we will."

"And why's that?"

"Because, among other things, I am stubborn as hell. And I have no intention of giving up on you, or on us, before we've even been given a real shot."

He smirked. "I'm okay with stubborn."

"Do you like me?" she asked, closing her eyes to prepare herself for the answer. "And I don't mean the idea of me. I mean the real me. Do you want to get to know that version?"

He held up his hand to stop her from rambling. "I do like you."

"Good," she said, taking a deep breath for what felt like the first time throughout the evening.

"Let's just go from there."

She agreed, leaning over and turning up the radio. A song was playing that she didn't recognize but she turned to him anyway. "What do you say to another dance?"

He nodded slightly, opening his door. "Don't get used to this," he told her, standing up out of his car. "You get this version of me for one night only."

"Of course." She smiled, meeting him in the headlights. He put his arms around her waist once more, pulling her closer than he had at the school. She could smell the cologne he was wearing—warm with a hint of leather. She laid her head on his chest, hearing his heartbeat under her ear. His body tensed under her weight slightly, but he kept moving. His face fell down to the side of hers, their cheeks brushing slightly. She could feel goosebumps growing on her arms as they swayed in place, their bodies moving together. The

stubble on his cheeks scratched hers and she shivered. He pulled back slightly, their faces only inches apart.

"Are you cold?" he asked. "I can get my jacket." His warm breath hit her cheeks and she watched the dark shadows dance across his stony face.

"It's not the cold," she said, shaking her head. He leaned in slightly, his lips finding hers. Her mouth opened on contact, allowing him to kiss her deeper. It was what she had been waiting for. The world around them seemed to spin faster as their kiss grew. Her stomach leapt into her chest at his touch, her heart pounding.

His kiss was soft at first. Cautious. His every move a question as to what was okay. But as her fingers found their way to his hair, pulling him to her passionately, he seemed to let loose, allowing their body heat to warm the night around them. Their kiss, his lips enveloping hers, was all that she had been dreaming of and as they stood, their bodies pressed together in the moonlight, nothing had ever felt more right.

FOURTEEN

GUNNER
PRESENT DAY

Gunner stood in Reagan's living room, a pink plastic dollhouse on the floor in front of him. The room was large, painted a rustic green and heavily clad with furniture and toys. Reagan re-entered the room, a mug of coffee in her hand. She offered it to him.

"Thanks," he said quietly, taking a sip and pretending it hadn't burned his mouth. Reagan pointed to the mantle, where a school picture of the little girl sat. Her wavy dark hair was pulled back in a headband, a tooth missing from her proud smile. Gunner stared into the bright green eyes that matched her mother's, surrounded by thick lashes. "She's beautiful," he told her honestly, running a finger over the frame.

"Thank you," she said.

"I'm sorry I wasn't here. If I had known..." He trailed off, not sure how to finish that sentence. He didn't know if that would've changed his mind back then.

"If you had known...what?" she asked, her voice unaccusing.

"I would've wanted to be a part of her life."

"But not mine?"

"Reagan—"

"I deserve an explanation, Gunner. Those were your words. I deserve to know the truth. God, do you have any idea what your disappearance did to me? How long I looked for you? Waited for you?"

"I never wanted to hurt you."

She sighed. "So what do you want? What do you want now? With Nora?"

"Does she know about me?" he asked softly, unable to meet her eye.

She pressed her lips together. "She knows you exist. Nothing more."

"I don't know if I'm ready to be a dad. We used protection that night—this is the last thing I expected when I came back to town. "

She crossed her arms. "No one's forcing you to do anything."

"What about you? You were eighteen years old. Were you ready?"

She shook her head. "This isn't about me, Gunner. It never was. That girl deserves my best and so I give it to her. That's all that counts."

"Do you need money?"

She frowned. "No. No, Gunner, we don't need your money. We don't have a lot, but we're good."

"I'm trying to do the right thing, Rae. I owe you money for her. I can't imagine how tough this has been on you...I just don't want to make any promises to you. I've only had a few minutes to process everything."

"You don't *have* to process anything. It was your choice to come here."

"She needs a father, Reagan."

"So, what are you suggesting?"

"Could I meet her?" he asked finally.

She seemed taken aback by his question. After a few moments, she spoke carefully. "I don't know."

"Okay," he said. He wasn't sure if he felt disappointment or relief.

"I don't want her to get hurt, Gunner."

"I don't want that either," he agreed.

She rested her hand on the mantle, taking a deep breath. "Could I have a day or two to figure everything out?"

"Of course."

"You're still planning on leaving?"

"I'm going back to New York, yes."

"Okay," she said, sadness surprising him as it filled her face. "Okay."

He sat the coffee mug down on the table, moving to touch her hand. "I'll respect whatever decision you make. It's your choice. I don't know that I'd be a good dad to her. I don't know if I'm even a good person for her to have in her life. But I'd like to try." He took in a sharp breath as his eyes met hers. "I'd love to try. I know I can't make up for the past eight years. I know I can't explain to her why I was gone. So, if you say no, I'll respect that. But just know...I'm willing to try if you are."

"Try?"

"Try to get to know our daughter."

"You believe she's yours?"

"I believe you if you say she is."

"She is, Gunner," she confirmed. "I know what you saw that night. But it wasn't what you think—"

He held his hand up. "I can't have that conversation. I need to process everything with Nora. She has to be priority. If you want to rehash everything in our past, we can plan to do that. On your terms."

"I'd like that," she said, a small smile on her face.

"All right. We'll make it happen then."

"Tonight?" she asked anxiously.

"I'm free." He nodded.

"Okay. I'll pick you up around..." He paused, looking to her for guidance.

"Make it six. I have to drop some stuff off for Nora at my parents' house. You can pick me up there."

He nodded. "Okay, I can do that." He turned to walk from the house, casting one last look at the girl he never thought he'd see again. Maybe there was hope after all.

FIFTEEN

REAGAN

MAY 2009

Reagan walked into the gymnasium, her eyes searching the crowd for him. She checked her phone, he hadn't texted her since he'd left work. She quickly found her seat next to her parents on the bleachers. Holly was there somewhere, but she hadn't seen her since they'd come in and she'd disappeared to be with her friends.

"Hey, Rae," Bethany Aarons said, sliding in beside her.

"Hey, Bethany," she said politely.

"Who are you here for?"

"Gunner's graduating," she replied stiffly.

"Ah, that's still a thing? So crazy," the girl said.

"Why's it crazy?" Reagan asked testily.

"Oh, no reason. You guys are cute together," she answered quickly, though Reagan could tell she wasn't being genuine.

"Who are you here for?"

"My brother."

"Oh, I didn't know he graduated this year. Wasn't he held back?"

Bethany stared at her, her lips tight. "Last year."

"Right," Reagan said, her heart racing. She was so tired of hearing other people's thoughts about her and Gunner. Since prom night, everyone seemed to have an opinion about them. Namely, why they shouldn't be together.

The graduation music began as their principal walked onto the stage and Reagan was thankful for a reason to end the conversation.

"Parents, family members, friends, alumni: the class of 2008 thanks you for coming tonight. We are so excited to see these students, these young minds that we've helped mold, as they go out into the world and help to change it. And, hopefully, make it better. Please welcome our graduates."

He stepped back from the podium as the music played again and the students, clad in their caps and gowns, entered the gymnasium. She spied Gunner pretty quickly and couldn't help but smile. His cap was pulled down, nearly covering his eyes and he couldn't have looked more annoyed. She'd basically had to force him to come to this 'stupid thing' but she was glad he'd finally agreed, and she hoped he would be too someday.

They took their seats and the principal began calling them up, one by one. When they called Gunner's name, Reagan looked for his family. Gavin was a few rows ahead of her, where she finally laid eyes on Holly, but Gia and his parents seemed to be missing. So much about Gunner's family was still a mystery to her.

She clapped extra loud for his row when they gave them

permission to and she winked when he caught her eye. He rolled his eyes playfully and she knew he was going to tease her for buying into such a cheesy ceremony, but she loved it. Truth was, she loved him. She couldn't admit it yet. Maybe she wouldn't ever be able to, but she felt it when she looked at him. Gunner had grown on her and she was loving every minute she spent with him.

WHEN THE CEREMONY ENDED, *Reagan rushed down the steps of the bleachers to meet him. He'd kept his cap, not bothering to throw it when the rest of his class did; he now held it under his arm.*

"Happy now?" he asked when he saw her.

"Yep," she teased. "You look so cute." She reached up, patting the top of his head.

"Shut up," he said, pretending to be annoyed.

Her parents approached them from behind her, her mother's hand on her back. "Congratulations, Gunner," she said politely.

"Thank you, Mrs. Orrick."

"Were your parents able to make it?" her father asked, looking around.

"No, sir. My dad wasn't feeling well."

"Well, I'm sorry to hear that. Gemma was hoping to finally meet your mother. I haven't seen her in years."

"She doesn't get out much," Gunner said quietly.

"Do you two have plans later? We'd be happy to take you out to dinner to celebrate if you'd like." Scott changed the subject quickly.

"Oh, no. Thank you for offering. I ate a big lunch so I'm not really hungry," he told them.

With that, her parents said their goodbyes and left the two of them alone.

"Do you have plans tonight?" she asked, feeling a bit disappointed.

"I thought about going to a party. Do you want to come?"

"To a party?"

"Yes. We don't have to. It was just a thought."

"No, it's fine. We just haven't been to a party together since..."

"I know," he said, stopping her from having to relive that night.

She twirled a piece of hair around her finger. "We can go."

He began unzipping his gown, pulling it off as fast as he could. "Do you need to tell your parents we're leaving?"

"They'll be all right," she said, waving to them over his shoulder. Her mother waved back, continuing to talk to one of the teachers.

"Okay, then, let's go." He walked from the gym, turning to make sure she was following him. He led her out of the building, the warm night air hitting them. The humidity made her hair cling to her neck immediately.

She climbed into his car, cranking the air conditioning as soon as she was settled in. "So, whose party is it?" she asked.

"Just an after party for graduation."

"Like, with kids in your class?"

"Well, yeah."

"Since when do you socialize with people in your class?" she asked, feeling impressed but shocked.

"I guess you're becoming a bad influence on me," he told her, patting her leg.

"Hm, somehow I doubt that. Hey, why didn't your parents come tonight?"

"I told you, my dad didn't feel good."

"What about your mom?"

"I don't know, Reagan. Why?"

"I still haven't been able to meet them. I just figured tonight would be my chance."

"Trust me, you aren't missing much."

"That can't be true. They raised this pretty awesome guy I know," she teased.

"It's not a big deal, Rae. Seriously."

She dropped the subject, sensing his agitation. His family was a very touchy subject for him and she'd learned to take whatever bits of information he was willing to give her.

They pulled up to a house that looked mostly empty. "I guess we're the first ones here," he said awkwardly, not stopping the car completely.

"Should we go in?" she asked.

"Nah, we'll make a few laps around town. We can come back once more people arrive."

"Okay," she said, feeling relieved.

"Are you okay?" he asked, sensing her nervousness.

"I'm fine," she assured him.

"You don't seem fine."

"I am, honestly."

"Okay," he said stiffly.

"I just...I haven't been to a party since that night."

He looked at her. "You haven't?"

"No," she said, feeling tears close to her eyelids.

"Reagan, we don't have to go."

"No, if it's important to you...I'll go."

"It's not important to me. You're important to me. I'm an idiot. I didn't think of how this would affect you. I'm so sorry."

"It's not your fault."

He rubbed a hand over the side of her face. "Don't ever be afraid to tell me something. You could've just said you didn't want to go."

"I didn't want to bum you out," she said simply.

"Rae, you're all I care about. You. I don't want to hurt you. So help me prevent that however I can."

"What are you going to do after this?" she asked him the question that had been weighing on her mind.

"What do you mean? Tonight?"

"Like for college?"

"Oh, I'm not going to college."

"You're not?"

"Don't look so surprised. You ought to have known that. I barely graduated."

"Well, you never really give me answers when I ask about your plans."

"Is that what this is about?" he asked.

"What?"

"You're worried about me leaving?"

"No," she said defensively.

"Yes, you are." He looked genuinely surprised.

"Well, is that such a bad thing?"

"I figured you'd be glad to be rid of me." He pulled the car over to the side of the road near a wheat field.

"I don't want to get rid of you."

"No?" he asked.

"No," she said seriously. "I really like spending time with you, Gunner. I care about you, too."

"Well, I don't plan on going anywhere anytime soon."

"Good."

He opened the car door. "Want to go for a walk?"

"In the field? Won't we get into trouble?"

"No one comes out here this late." Without having to be coaxed further, Reagan stepped out of the car. She took his hand, letting him lead her to the edge of the field. "You'll graduate next year."

She nodded. "I know."

"Will you go somewhere?"

She stared at him. "Are you asking?"

"I'm asking," he told her, looking straight ahead.

She grinned broadly. "I don't know what I'll do yet. I could stay around here."

"A lot could change between now and then."

"A lot could."

"We could change," he told her.

"But we could not.*"*

"Maybe not." He pulled her into the field.

"Gunner?" she called his name, watching him move through the shadows, his hand holding hers.

"Yeah?" He stopped.

"I hope we don't change."

He didn't respond, pulling her further into the darkness. She pushed the stalks of wheat out of her way, trying to keep up. Finally, the field ended and they were standing near a pond. The moon reflected off the water, making her smile.

"Let's swim," he said.

"Did you know this was here?" she asked.

He shrugged, pulling his shirt over his head and slipping out of his pants and shoes. He ran down the dock, jumping into the water without another word, splashing loudly as he landed. It was rare that she saw him so carefree and so she didn't want to worry him with questions about who might catch them. She pulled the zipper of her dress down, and slipped her heels off. She eased the dress over her hips and laid it on the ground, walking cautiously toward him.

"Woah, slow down there, Grandma," he joked as she tiptoed into the cool water.

"There could be snakes," she told him.

"There could've been snakes in the field, too."

"Don't remind me." She shivered, making her way to him.

He wrapped his arms around her, rubbing his palms over her shoulders in an attempt to warm her. "I'll protect you," he said.

She laid her head on his chest. "You always do."

"I'll always do whatever I can for you, Reagan. I just hope that's enough," he said, his jaw tight, eyes locked on hers as she looked up at him.

"You're more than enough, Gunner. You always will be," she said breathlessly.

He leaned down, pulling her chin up so their lips could meet. His kiss was soft, his facial hair scratching her skin. She touched his hands carefully as they began to caress her face. His hands traveled across her body, fingers running along her sides and down her back slowly. Her heart pounded as he touched places he hadn't touched before. She pulled away, unable to catch her breath.

"Are you okay?" he asked.

"I'm okay," she assured him.

He splashed her and she laughed. "I can see your blush even in the moonlight."

"I'm not blushing."

"You are."

She splashed him back. "Well, I've never been this...undressed...with you."

He twisted his mouth, looking as though he were thinking. "So you haven't."

She shook her head.

"Do I make you nervous?" he asked, running a hand along her bare back once again.

"Yes," she said firmly.

"Is that a bad thing?"

She looked him in the eye though her body trembled at his touch. "I don't think so."

"You know nothing is going to happen tonight," he whispered, his hand still on her skin.

"I know."

*"Nothing besides...*this!*" he screamed, dunking her underwater. She shot back up, sucking in a deep breath. She hadn't been prepared to go underwater but the happy look on his face made her smile.*

"You jerk." She turned to walk away from him, rubbing her eyes. "You almost made me lose a contact."

He picked her up from behind, spinning her around. His lips were on the back of her neck. "I'm sorry," he told her, his breath warming her skin.

She turned in his grasp, her arms encircling his neck. "You'd better be."

"You are truly something else, Reagan."

"I pride myself in that."

His mouth was on hers again, lifting her up so her legs wrapped around his waist. She was very aware that the only thing between them was her bra and panties. Her skin pressed against his, the water making them stick together. He held her tight, his tongue exploring her mouth. She took a breath, her hands moving to his hair. She ran her fingers through the long locks, her pulse pounding through every part of her body. She slid down his front as he let her go, his hands moving lower down her back. He reached the top of her pantyline and stopped, stepping back.

"We have to stop."

She nodded but leaned up to kiss him again. He held her at arm's length. "I'm serious, Rae. If we don't stop now, I'm afraid I won't be able to later." He took her hand in his, walking to the shore and sitting in the dirt, his wetness causing mud to form around him instantly. She sank down beside him.

"I'm sorry," she told him.

"You have no reason to be sorry," he insisted.

"You're so much more experienced than I am. I know it's hard on you having to wait on me."

"It's not so bad."

"You don't want to do it?" She felt offended.

He leaned his head back, sighing deeply. "You have no idea how badly I want to do it." He looked at her, his face serious. "But you mean more to me than that. You mean more to me than any girl I've ever been with. And I'm not just saying that because it's what you're supposed to say, trust me. I'm fine with waiting. I want your first time to be special, Rae.

You're too special to have it be anything else. I want it to be when you're ready. Even if that isn't with me."

"I hope it's with you," she whispered.

"I hope so too," he told her, kissing her hand. "Someday. But, for now, this is perfect. Everything, anything with you...is perfect."

SIXTEEN

REAGAN

July 2010

Reagan sat on her front porch, her bare feet rubbing the hot, concrete walkway. She heard his car before she saw it, her heart picking up speed as he neared. She skipped to the edge of the yard, the sun beating down on her exposed shoulders. He pulled up, his car coming to a stop, and smiled at her.

"What are you doing here?" she asked. "I thought you were working all week."

He shrugged his shoulders, smirking. "I took a few days off. What are you doing right now?"

"Oh, I don't know," she said, leaning down to kiss his lips. "Why?"

"My grandparents are out of town for the week. I thought we could go up to their house on the lake for the afternoon."

"What? I thought you never went there. Will your parents be okay with it?"

"I'm supposed to be working on the boat all day. They'll never know the difference."

She thought for a moment before smiling excitedly. "Okay, I'm in. Let me go grab some things and tell Holly I'm leaving."

"Bring a bathing suit," he called after her as she turned to walk away.

"Obviously," she threw the word over her shoulder.

He laughed out loud, his laugh warming her even more than the one-hundred-degree summer. She heard it so rarely. As she ran into the house, she grabbed her cellphone from the coffee table.

"Holly!" she yelled.

Her sister stuck her head out of her bedroom door just as Reagan had reached the top of the staircase.

"Where's the fire?" her sister asked sarcastically.

"I'm going out."

"Out where?"

"Gunner's taking me to the lake. I'll text mom to let her know, but I won't be back until later. Are you guys okay here?"

Gavin could suddenly be seen beside her, a smug grin on his face. "That slick son of a bitch. Of course he's going to the lake house the second it's empty."

"Uh, you have a lake house?" Holly looked to Gavin.

"It's not ours. It's our grandparents' and we're never allowed to go there. But, they just happen to be out of town."

"No fair," she whined. "I want to go!"

"Me too," Gavin played along, staring at Reagan with a mockingly pouty face.

"Don't you two have better things to do than tag along with the grown-ups?"

Gavin chuckled loudly, placing his elbow on the top of her head as if she were an armrest. He looked down at her, showing off his height. "You aren't so grown up, Rae."

She tossed a towel at him from the closet on her right. "Well, if you can convince your brother, I don't care if you guys third and fourth wheel with us." Holly clapped her hands together, her eyes lighting up. "But hurry up, we're leaving now." She turned from them, walking into her room. She grabbed a tote bag, throwing a tube of chapstick, phone charger, sunglasses, and a hairbrush into it. She walked to her dresser, digging through it to find her favorite bikini. She pulled her clothes off, sliding the suit on and then redressing. She threw a clean pair of panties and bra into the bag as well, turning and darting from the room as she sent her mother a quick text.

When she got out of the house, Gavin and Holly were already in Gavin's truck, a small black s10 that looked like it might not make it across town let alone the two hour trek it would take to get to the lake. Her eyes moved to Gunner, who was sitting in his car with a sour look on his face.

"You invited Gavin along?" he asked when she climbed into the passenger's seat.

"Well, not as much as he invited himself." She grinned as Gavin fired up the engine and peeled out of the driveway, winking at her before speeding off. The truck disappeared in an instant. She rolled her eyes, shaking her head and turning to Gunner. He started his car up, not returning her stares, and began following them. He stayed several feet behind, not both-

ering to speed up in order to stay with Gavin. For most of the ride, he was strangely quiet.

"I'm really excited about this," she said, breaking the silence. "I've always wanted to spend the afternoon at your grandparents' lake house."

"Yeah," he said softly, turning down a small street that led to Montgomery County.

"Is everything all right?" she asked after a few more silent moments had passed.

He blinked, seemingly out of his trance. "What? Oh, yeah. I'm fine."

"You don't seem fine. I hope you aren't mad that I said they could come."

"I'm not mad at you," he assured her, moving his hand from the steering wheel to squeeze hers. "It's just...my brother isn't exactly my idea of good company."

"He's your brother. I couldn't just say no."

"Yeah," he said, his voice strained. She could tell she had touched a nerve. "No one can say no to Gavin."

"Did I do something wrong? I can tell them never mind. We can think up an excuse."

He shook his head, offering up a small smile. "I'm fine. Don't worry about me."

She squeezed his hand back, her other arm dangling out the window. Everything was fine, he'd said, and so she assured herself it would be.

ONCE THEY'D ARRIVED *at the lake, the hostile vibe had completely disappeared and to her surprise Gunner looked genuinely happy as he ushered her into the house. The sun shone in the large windows and the lake could be seen just feet away.*

Holly groaned behind them. "I need to be in that water."

On cue, Gavin ripped off his t-shirt, dropping his phone in the nearest chair and darting out the back door. "Come on!" he screamed, Holly following close behind him.

Gunner remained behind, Reagan noticed his eyes rolling slightly. Reagan picked up their clothes from the floor, sighing. "Kids these days," she joked, sinking down into a wooden rocking chair. The lakehouse had a rustic feel: wooden paneling throughout and tall, airy ceilings. She looked around at the many taxidermied animals that adorned the walls.

Gunner came to stand in front of her, his hand brushing her knee. "Come on," he said, his palm outstretched.

"Where are we going?" she asked, her eyes darting to the windows. "With them?"

"Nope."

"Then where?"

"You'll see," he told her. "It's a surprise."

She stood up, her hand in his as he led her out the door they'd entered through. "Where are you taking me?" she asked again as they descended the big hill the house was perched upon.

"Don't you worry your pretty little head," he said playfully. They entered the edge of the woods and he pulled a ring of keys from his back pocket, jingling them. They walked toward an old shed and he placed a key into a rusted padlock.

"So, is this where you kill me?"

He laughed, twisting the key. "Nah, too messy." He swung open the heavy wooden door, pulling a tan blanket off something in the center of the room and revealing an old four wheeler.

"Are you going to take me for a ride?" she asked gleefully. It had been years since she'd rode one.

"That was the plan." He nodded, walking into the shed and grabbing a towel from the wall to wipe the cobwebs and dust off the ATV. Even with the cover, it was filthy.

"Do you guys come up here often?" From the looks of the building, the answer was no.

He coughed, blinking as dust flew into his eyes. "No, not in years. Mom isn't welcome anymore. Dad never was. We used to spend summers up here but the older we got...the more trouble we caused and the less they trusted us."

"Do they know we're here now?" she asked.

"No," he said, patting the seat a few more times and laying the towel on a workbench. "They gave Gia a key a few years ago. Out of everyone, she's the one they trust the most. Plus, I think they hoped if things ever got too bad at home, she'd come here. Anyway, Gia let it slip that they left on a cruise for the week so I saw an opportunity to give you a vacation and ran with it."

"So, they're your mom's parents, then? Or your dad's?"

"My mom's," he answered, and then, sensing what her question actually was, he went on. "They're good people. Mom wasn't raised the way we are. She met my dad at, like, fifteen. Everyone knew he was nothing but trouble, according to my grandparents, but she didn't care. My grandparents will never forgive her for marrying him."

"I'm so sorry, Gunner." She couldn't imagine what sort of people would tell a child that about his own parents.

He shrugged. "No need to be sorry. I've never known any

different." He grabbed a nearby gas can, shaking it to determine if it was empty. When he realized it wasn't, he began topping off the tank. "Now, climb aboard, princess."

She groaned loudly. "I thought we'd moved past the whole princess thing."

"Never ever," he promised, taking her arm and helping her climb onto the seat. He climbed on behind her, his arms wrapping around her to grab the handles. He started it up. The rumble of the engine echoed through the quiet woods. He put it in reverse and pulled them out of the barn with ease, dust flying all around them. His body enveloped her. She held tightly to the black bar that ran in front of the seat, his arms making her feel safe. He placed his head near hers.

"Hold on tight," he warned her over the noise as their speed began to increase. They flew over bumps and hills, spinning quickly around trees and curves. She laughed, carefree and completely happy, as the world around them blurred by. He kissed her cheek. "Having fun?" he asked, his lips brushing her ear.

She nodded, the wind catching her voice as she tried to speak. He turned the four wheeler down a small trail, slowing down. "Where are we going now?" she asked, finding her voice. She ran a quick hand through her frazzled hair.

"Oh, all the questions..." he teased. "You'll just have to be patient." As he said it, they were stopping at the edge of the woods, their destination evident. The path had led them to a small, private section of the lake. The spot was serene; they were the only people around for what could've been miles.

He slid off of the seat, helping her down before removing his black t-shirt. His pale chest, smaller and less defined than Gavin's, glistened with sweat in the sun. She couldn't help but stare at him. She pulled her own clothes off quickly, revealing her yellow bikini. Together, they walked into the murky lake, its cool temperature surprising her. His eyes danced over her bare skin, though he tried to hide it, and she couldn't help but smile.

Each step they took splashed a bit of water onto them, mud squishing between her toes. She sank down, letting the water wash over her. "I can't believe we haven't come to this place before. I could spend every day here."

He smiled, tossing a handful of water her way. "We'll have to make sure you get here more often, then."

"I'd like that," she told him, taking his hand and placing it on her waist. She threw her legs up, her arms going around his neck. "Catch me!" she cried. He seemed surprised, but jumped into action quickly, baring her weight with ease. "How'd you find this place anyway?" she asked, running a finger along his bicep.

"I used to come out here a lot during the summers we stayed with my grandparents. I cleared the path myself. Sometimes, I just needed a place to get away from everything...everyone." He stared off into space, remembering.

"From Gia and Gavin?"

"From everything," he said stiffly, spinning her around so that ripples began to form around them.

"Your relationship with them is strange," she told him. It wasn't a question.

"It's...complicated." He nodded in confirmation.

"Too complicated to tell your girlfriend?"

He paused and she felt the tension growing. In the nearly two years since prom, he'd never once called her his girlfriend, though that was what she considered herself to be.

Gunner kept her, like everything else, at arm's length. Though they'd been technically dating for well over a year, there was still a wall between them—a wall she spent every day trying to tear down. Every once in a while, as if a brick had broken loose, he'd open up to her and let her see a side of him the rest of the world rarely did. He'd admitted to her, despite their distance, she was the closest person to him, and she had to take whatever he'd give her without demanding much more.

"You don't want to hear our family drama, trust me."

She frowned, climbing out of his arms and staring at him. "I tell you about all my fights with Holly. I'm sure that's not the most interesting part of your day."

"This is different, Rae," he said, moving a piece of hair that had stuck to her cheek.

"I don't care," she insisted. "I still want to know. You know I'm here for you, Gunner." She pressed her hands onto his chest. He stared at her, his eyes darting between hers and she could see him considering his next move—deciding whether he could trust her with his secrets. "Talk to me," she coaxed.

"You don't know what you're asking."

"Nothing you could possibly say will scare me off." She focused her gaze on him, begging him to trust her.

"You say that now." He pressed his lips together in disbelief.

She stood on her tiptoes, kissing his lips. He softened slightly. "Gunner," she whispered, her heart pounding. "I'm in love with you." His eyes grew wide, his face not bothering to hide his bewilderment. He didn't speak. "I'm in love with you," she repeated. "So, you can tell me anything. Because I'm not going anywhere." She remained still, waiting for him to respond.

"You shouldn't love me, Reagan," he said finally, looking away.

"Because you don't feel the same way?"

He sighed. "Because I'm going to end up disappointing you."

"You couldn't," she said, shaking her head and trying to understand.

He pulled back from her, turning and walking out of the water. When he reached the place where their clothes lay, he sat down, waiting for her. She followed him, sitting down next to him on the sandy shore. He reached over to where he'd thrown his jeans, pulling out a pack of cigarettes and a lighter and sticking a cigarette to his lips.

"Gunner, I don't know all your secrets. I don't know what horrible things have happened to you. I do know that despite it all, I love you. No matter what you say, I love you. The world may be dark and it may have hurt you. But I won't. I'm here for you, even if you think you've got this on your own. Even if you think it'll make you look weak to talk about the bad stuff...I'm still going to be here."

"It's not always about the world, Reagan."

"What do you mean?"

"Sometimes the stuff that happens at home is worse than the world could ever be. Sometimes our parents fuck us up before the world ever has its shot."

"What are you talking about?" she asked, horror filling her expression. The truth in his voice broke her heart before he could start to explain.

Inhaling deeply, he began to speak. "Gavin and Gia are

my half-siblings. Different dads." Reagan was quiet despite the outright shock she felt. *"Mom had an affair shortly after she had me. I don't know most of the details but Gavin and Gia were a result. They've never met their father—Rick's the only dad they've ever known, but the fact that they aren't his...it's just there, you know? Just hanging over all of us all the time. Rick hates them for it. Hates Mom, too. I don't remember a lot from the time before they were born but I don't think it was like it is now."*

"I'm sorry," she said, feeling like she should say something.

"Out of everyone, I have it the easiest," he said, shrugging. *"He's never laid a hand on me. It's Gavin and Gia that bear the brunt of his anger."*

"He hurts them?"

He nodded. "Bad sometimes. Broken bones. Bruises. Stitches—you name it, they've gotten it. And sometimes, they haven't gotten stitches or X-rays when they truly needed 'em. I can remember when I was little, they'd make them go without food. I always got some and Gavin and Gia would beg me to share but if I did, I'd be the one in trouble. My home is a war zone. Constantly. My dad is a bully, worse than anything I've ever seen. Mom's scared of him. Too scared to stand up and stop it. And it never happens when I'm around, but when I find out, it's always too late. They won't let me help them no matter what I try. Gavin's a big guy, but he won't stand up to him, and they won't talk to anyone about it. They just both want Rick to love them so much...they won't talk about what he does, won't admit the truth. Not to anyone."

"Oh, Gunner, you have to stop him. You have to tell the police." Tears filled her eyes as she pictured his life, a life like

something she'd only ever read about, had nightmares about. Even with her suspicions, she'd never imagined it could be so bad.

"No," he snapped quickly. "No. I've tried, believe me. No one would tell the truth. Not even Momma. I was made to look like an idiot the last time and then their beatings got worse. It'd be useless."

"No. That can't be true. Something has to be able to get done. There are people who can help them."

"It is true, Reagan. I didn't want to tell you for this very reason. You're still so full of...hope, faith, whatever. You believe everything can be fixed. But not everything can. This can't be fixed. You have to promise me you won't say anything. Not to anyone." His voice was firm, letting her know it wasn't up for discussion. He smashed the cigarette butt into the sand.

"Gunner, I—"

"I'm trusting you. You asked me to tell you the truth, and so, I have. Don't break my trust."

"I won't," she told him, her stomach in knots.

"Promise me, Reagan. You have to promise me you'll never tell anyone what I've told you."

"I promise."

"I only stayed around after graduation for them. And for Momma. But, once they graduate, I'll be gone."

"You'll leave Dale?" she asked, her heart plummeting at his words. Her true question hung in the air: you'll leave me? They hadn't discussed him leaving since the night of his graduation.

"I know I told you I had no plans to go anywhere. But things have changed. It's getting worse at home. I can't stick

around much longer. There's nothing here for me anymore, Rae."

"Not me?"

He shook his head. "You'll be fine. You're going off to college in the fall. You'll meet a guy like Gavin and you won't look back. I have to prepare myself for that. I don't want to be the thing that holds you back."

"Gunner, that's not true, you aren't holding me back. And I don't want any of that," she said seriously.

"You don't know that. Not yet."

"I'm not leaving Dale," she told him, watching his eyes change at her words. "More than that, I'm not leaving you. I don't want some pig-headed boy like your brother."

He looked away, his jaw tight. "And if I go?"

"I don't know." She bit her lip in thought.

"You'd stay," he confirmed.

She was silent for a moment, choosing her words carefully. "Dale is my home. I want to tell you that if you go, I go...but I don't want to lie to you unless I'm sure I could do that. I'd have to take some time to think."

"I don't want you to make sacrifices for me."

She pursed her lips. "You're the only one around here who gets to do that?"

"I would sacrifice anything for you," he said. His eyes were soft as he stared at her, the truth of his statement evident.

"You love me," she told him, a smile growing on her face.

"What?" he said, leaning back from her.

"I told you I love you and you didn't say it back...which is okay, because I know what I signed up for when I fell for you. You've got your wall ten feet high and armed against anyone who tries to get close. But, you love me. I can tell it in the way

you talk to me. I can see it in your eyes. I've learned to understand what you aren't saying."

He shook his head. "You are...completely crazy. And unlike anything or anyone I've ever known."

"But I'm not wrong."

"No," he admitted, "you're not wrong." He smiled, cupping her face in his hands and pressing his lips onto hers. He pulled away, resting his forehead on hers, their eyes locked together. "I'm scared one day you're going to wake up and realize you're with the wrong guy."

She touched her lips to his lightly, her hands going to his hair. He laid back on the sandy shore, pulling her on top of him. "I'm in love with you, Gunner James," she told him in between kisses. "And that makes you the right guy. I don't care about our families or the school or our friends or anything else. I determine who the right guy for me is...and you're it. So, love me back. And don't be afraid. Because love doesn't have to be scary. I'm never going to hurt you."

He pulled her close again, fire igniting in their kisses. He ran his hands through her wet hair and down her back, gripping her waist tight. She slid further down onto his chest until all her weight was resting on him, his skin hot against hers.

When their kiss finally ended, she pulled back slightly, staring down at him. "This was your plan all along, huh? Get me out here all alone so you could seduce me?" She laughed.

He smirked. "You know me so well." He leaned forward, kissing her neck sweetly and moving to sit up, keeping her on his lap.

She kissed him again, her tongue exploring his mouth. His fingers played with the strings of her bikini, causing her heart to pound harder. She could feel her pulse in her fingertips.

He pulled her hair gently, his lips finding her neck again. She sighed with pleasure. "I love you," his voice came in a soft whisper. She pulled away, staring at him with wide eyes. She wasn't sure she'd heard it, though she'd been waiting for so long. He smiled, kissing her nose. "Don't act so surprised. I've loved you from the very first time we committed truancy together. I just never thought that day would lead to this one."

"But you're glad it did?" she asked doubtingly.

"Yes," he assured her. "I'm very glad it did." He pulled at a tendril of her yellow hair playfully.

"Do you plan on leaving me anytime soon?"

"I don't want to stay in Dale," he told her seriously, "but I do want to be with you."

"So what do we do?"

"We leave that problem for our future selves. Today, I just want to relax and enjoy being here."

She kissed him again. "Sounds like a good plan to me."

SEVENTEEN

REAGAN

July 2010

Later that evening, the four teens sat on the deck of the lakehouse, enjoying the sunset. Holly rested her head on Gavin's shoulder, both their faces bright red from spending too much time in the sun.

Reagan and Gunner sat at the patio table, her fingers laced through his. "I don't ever want to leave this place," she said to no one in particular.

"I don't ever want to leave this spot," Holly chimed in.

Gavin spoke up, elbowing Holly playfully. "Hey, you want something to drink? I'll bet Grandpa keeps some good alcohol here. Expensive stuff."

Gunner shook his head. "No. We don't need to get into their alcohol. We don't want them to know we were here, remember?"

"Come on, Gun. Don't be a buzzkill," Gavin said pointedly and Reagan could see the anger growing in Gunner.

"You have to drive home later," Gunner said, keeping his temper in check.

"Or I could let you drive us home. We could come back and get my truck tomorrow. Everyone knows you aren't going to take a drink."

"Don't be a dick," Gunner said sharply.

"We could stay," Holly offered, easing the tension. Everyone turned to look at her.

"What?" Gavin asked.

"I mean...Reagan's eighteen. We could stay overnight. Mom and Dad trust her. As long as she's here, we could stay."

"I don't know, Hol," Reagan said nervously.

Gavin, not needing further assurance, stood up and disappeared into the house. He returned a few moments later, a bottle of whiskey and four tumblers in his hands. "I even brought you one, Brother," he said, a charming smile on his face.

They were all silent as Gavin filled the glasses. Reagan looked at Gunner, feeling uncomfortable. "If we stay, what will you tell your parents?"

"They won't ask," Gunner answered quietly, not looking at anyone.

"Hell, they won't notice. Two less mouths to feed," Gavin said loudly. He picked up his glass, clinking it to an imaginary one in the air and gulping the dark liquid down. Holly moved to pick up her own glass.

"It's fine, Rae," she assured her sister. "I'll text Mom and Dad."

Reagan bit her lip, feeling uneasy. "Tell them the truth, Hol. No lies."

"I won't lie," she said, pulling her phone out of her back pocket and beginning to type a message.

Reagan looked to Gunner. "Are you okay with this? I don't mind staying, but I don't mind leaving either."

The clenched fists he held on the glass tabletop told her he wasn't. "You are welcome to stay," he said stiffly, still not looking her way. "If you're comfortable with it. I don't want you to do anything you don't want to."

She nodded. "I'm okay with it," she said, trying to reassure him. She reached up, pushing her glass away. "But I don't want to drink if you aren't."

He moved his hand to squeeze hers. "You can if you want. It's a personal choice for me. It has nothing to do with you."

"I don't want to," she promised.

"More for me," Gavin exclaimed obnoxiously, combining their drinks into his glass. Holly took a sip of hers, smiling brightly as she slipped the phone back into her pocket.

"Pace yourself," Reagan warned them.

Gavin sighed dramatically. "Come on, Holly. Let's leave these two losers alone to wallow in their self-loathing. They're bringing me down."

Holly let him pull her down the porch steps and Reagan felt a sense of relief as they disappeared from sight. She turned to face him. "Gunner, I can go home if you want me to. I can make Holly go home. I feel like you aren't comfortable with this."

He frowned. "I love spending time with you, Rae. I don't want you to think I don't. And I'm always okay with spending a night away from my parents. But I don't want you to feel pressured to...do anything."

She sucked in a breath, realizing the cause of his sudden awkwardness. "Oh. You're worried we'll have sex?"

He turned slightly in his chair so he was facing her. "I'm not worried. I just want it to be done on your terms, like I've always said. I don't want Gavin to influence you because he can't control himself around free alcohol. I don't want you to think being here means you're obligated to be with me. I know how important waiting is to you. It's why I've tried not to pressure you."

"So, if I told you I'm planning to wait until I'm married?" she asked, her eyebrows raised.

His response was instant; his expression told her he wasn't surprised. "That's a decision you have to make. It doesn't change how I feel about you."

"That you love me," she reminded him.

He smiled warmly, letting out a breath. "It doesn't change the fact that I love you."

"Do you want to go for a walk?" Reagan asked suddenly.

"A walk in the woods at night?" His forehead wrinkled in shock.

"What? Are you scared?" she asked, joy filling her voice.

"Yeah, right," he said, scoffing at her. "Actually, I have something else I want to show you." He stood up, taking her hand. They walked down the hill and into the dark woods. The ground beneath their feet crackled and crunched with their every step.

She was silent, one thought running through her mind over and over again. It was sitting on the tip of her tongue and yet she couldn't bring herself to say it. Finally, he stopped, pointing to a tall tree, a treehouse sat at the top. "Look."

"What's that?" she asked, trying to make it out in the moonlight.

"My grandpa built it for my mom when she was little. They typically spent their summers out here. We played up there a lot as kids."

"It's fantastic. I always wanted something like this," she told him happily. "Can we climb up there?"

He tapped the wooden ladder, pulling on the steps to test them. "Let me see if it'll hold my weight. There's no telling how long it's been since anyone's been up there."

She nodded. "Be careful."

He put a foot on the first step, leaning his weight on it before he began climbing cautiously. She held her breath as she watched him ascend. When he reached the top, climbing into the fort with a loud THUD, he turned around, dusting his hands off and nodding. "Come on up."

She smiled, grabbing ahold of the first step and pulling herself up. The hard, rough wood was bowed and dry but it held her weight well. She climbed carefully, reaching out for his hand and letting him pull her the rest of the way up.

Once she was inside, she looked around the fort, wiping her hands on her shorts. The room was bare, the walls still had studs visible from the inside, and yet it felt quaint. In the moonlight, she could make out writing along the boards: signatures, height markers, and drawings.

"This place is so cool," she said, trying to picture a younger Gunner playing here.

"It used to be," he said. "It's nothing special now." She walked to look out one of the tiny windows and felt his arms

surround her. He nuzzled into her neck. "What's one thing you want to do before you die?"

"Because you're about to kill me?" she asked.

He laughed softly. "Seriously. One thing. Bucket list."

She thought for a moment, then giggled. "I want to learn to fly a helicopter."

She could feel his smile growing, his cheeks pressing against hers. "Why's that?"

"I don't know. It's just something I've always wanted to learn to do."

"Are you going to give rides around Dale?" he teased.

She shook her head. "Only for you."

He kissed her cheek, his lips remaining on her skin for a moment longer than usual. "I'll stay for you," he whispered in her ear, his breath warm against her face.

She gasped, turning her head to look at him. "In Dale?"

"If that's what you want."

She was facing him then. She wrapped her arms around him, breathing him in. When she pulled away, she rubbed her thumbs over his eyebrows, staring at him intently. "I'll leave for you, too."

"You will?" he asked, his voice raised, obviously not expecting her to say that.

"I want to be with you, Gunner. Anywhere. Any way. And, if that means we leave Dale, we do. I want you to be happy."

He rubbed a piece of stray hair from her cheeks. "So, you want to stay and I want to go," he said softly.

"And you're willing to stay, but I'm willing to go." She nodded.

"Well, where does that leave us?" he asked.

She smiled at him, sliding her hand onto his cheek. "Right here." She leaned forward, touching her lips to his lightly. Her heart fluttered in her chest, cold chills running up and down her spine. She wrapped her hands around his neck, pulling him to her. His hands were around her waist instantly, his fingers gripping her tight as their kisses grew.

He pushed her backward gently, and she took a deep breath as her skin met the wall. Their lips parted for just a moment and he smiled at her, his eyes searching hers. She ran her hands over his shoulders, the soft cotton of his t-shirt under her fingertips, and pulled his face down so she could taste his lips again. Her whole body pulsed with his every move. His hands moved from her hips, sliding carefully under her shirt. His palms were cold on her bare back. He moved his mouth to her neck, her body reacting immediately. Her body ached for him. She felt the hardness in his pants growing, his excitement for her evident. He searched for her mouth again, their bodies pressed firmly together as his kiss overwhelmed her.

"I love you," she whispered heatedly.

"I love you, Reagan," he repeated, his voice serious. She pulled away, reaching for the bottom of her shirt. She pulled it up, removing it quickly. He looked her over, his eyes filled with desire. His lips went to her bare skin immediately, his kisses dancing around her bra. She breathed nervously, feeling like her heart may explode. With shaking hands, she moved to his waist, her fingers fumbling with his belt.

He cupped her breasts, his breath hot on her chest and she moaned as he slid his hands under her bra. She started to undo the button on his pants, her hands shaking fiercely, but he stopped her.

"What are you doing?" he asked breathlessly. It was the line they hadn't crossed. The stopping point up until now. They'd come close many times...too close on his graduation night and then even closer on hers, but she hadn't been ready.

She felt ready now though, and it wasn't just the hormones talking. She had vowed to never let her hormones make this decision for her. But this time it was her heart giving the go-ahead.

"I'm ready, Gunner." He'd told her he loved her. And he'd done it in a way that she could believe it was true. She had decided long ago she wasn't going to give herself to someone who would say whatever it took to get in her pants and Gunner had proven time and time again he wouldn't be that guy.

He pulled his hands from her breasts, moving them to her hips, his face still inches from hers. "You said you wanted to wait until you were married."

The corners of her mouth turned up slightly. "I wanted to see how you'd react."

"I don't care about sex, Rae. I don't want you to think that waiting will change us or how I feel about you. I can wait as long as you need me to. I don't want to pressure you." His breathing was heavy.

"You aren't," she assured him. "I've thought about this. A lot actually. I'm ready."

"Are you sure?" he asked, his eyes lighting up. She reveled in how happy he seemed.

"I am," she told him confidently, though she felt anything but. "But I'm nervous."

"You don't have to be nervous," he told her, hugging her

tight. "I'll be gentle." He let out a small, nervous laugh. "And we can stop if you change your mind."

"Okay," she said, nodding. She reached behind her, starting to unclasp her bra.

"Wait." He touched her arm, pulling her hands to her sides. "Not here. No way am I letting your first time be in a mildewy old tree house filled with ants and pinecones."

"I don't care where we are."

"I do," he said, bending over and grabbing her shirt from the ground. He shook it off before handing it back to her. "I care because I care about you. And I care about this memory. I'm not letting this be it for you. Let's go back to the house."

She threw her shirt over her head, unsure of what to say. He helped her down the ladder and out of the woods quickly, both of them lost in their own thoughts. When they made it back to the house, it was empty. She sighed with relief, not sure she could've gone through with any of it if she'd had to see Gavin and Holly.

"You still okay?" he asked, squeezing her hand.

She looked down the long hallway to where she assumed the bedrooms must be. "Yes," she whispered, following him as he began walking through the living room. Waves of excitement and nervousness rushed over her as he opened the second door and flipped on the light. The small bedroom had an old wooden bed inside of it. A white quilt and lace pillows covered the mattress.

"Breathe," he instructed her and she let out a breath she hadn't been consciously holding in. He smiled, walking to the bed and sitting down. She tried desperately to calm her nerves, following his lead as he patted the comforter, waiting for her.

"This doesn't have to happen tonight," he told her, making fierce eye contact.

She nodded. "Do you want it to?"

"It doesn't matter what I want. This is about you."

"It matters to me," she whispered, feeling cool tears in her eyes.

"I've wanted to do this for a very long time," he said, "but if I'm being honest...I'm terrified. Maybe more than you."

"You are?" she asked, unable to hide her surprise.

He ran a finger over her leg. "Some days I'm still waiting to wake up and realize this was all some dream. I am terrified we'll do this and I'll somehow mess up this moment for you. I want it to be everything you want...but that's a lot of pressure on me."

"It's just sex, Gunner." She shrugged casually, trying to seem more aloof than she felt.

"No," he insisted, wiping away her first tear as it fell. "No, it'll never be just sex with you. Trust me...when we do it, if we do it, *it will be something special. You, Reagan, you deserve for it to be special."*

She leaned forward, more sure of her decision than ever as their lips collided. The universe seemed to stop spinning and nothing else mattered. No one else existed but the two of them. She laid back on the bed carefully, allowing him to pull her shirt over her head.

"If you change your mind—"

"You'll be the first to know," she promised him, pulling his shirt off quickly. Their bare skin pressed into each other's, Reagan's body felt as though it were on fire. His hands moved carefully over her bra straps, pulling them off her shoulders so

her breasts were exposed. He lowered himself so his mouth found them, her eyes rolling back in pleasure.

She felt him fidgeting with her shorts, his thumb rolling over the button. He slid the zipper down easily and she lifted her hips, helping him to remove them, her eyes locked on his.

She nodded, assuring him it was still okay. She was really doing this. He slid a hand between her legs, causing her to squirm. Everything he did to her felt amazing. Her body pulsed electricity: every hair stood on end, every inch of skin carried its own heartbeat. To her dismay, his hand stopped moving, and she opened her eyes.

Don't stop, *she wanted to beg, but she remained silent, staring at him wildly.*

"Still okay?" he asked again, his hands on his own belt as he stood up. She looked over his bare chest, nodding. As he pulled his pants down, she leaned forward, trying to calm her racing thoughts. She pressed her lips to his chest, wanting to taste every inch of him. He pulled his boxers down slowly and her eyes traveled to the part of him she'd spent so long imagining. She reached out, her hand taking hold of him as he pulsed under her fingers.

He laid her back onto the bed once more, moving the covers down and allowing her to crawl under them. He pulled a purple wrapper from the wallet in his pants pocket and tore it open.

"I'll go slow," he swore to her as he slid the condom over himself. "You can stop me if you need to." She nodded, reaching for his skin again and pulling him to her. "I love you," he reminded her as he inched under the covers. He kissed her forehead, nose, and finally her mouth. His kisses were delicate as they both shook with adrenaline, their

breathing uneasy. His hand was between her legs and she felt him slide his knee in between hers.

"I love you back," she told him as their lips separated.

"This may hurt a little," he warned her. She wanted to say something witty, like 'well, someone's sure of himself' but nerves got the best of her and she could only smile nervously.

She felt his hand guiding himself closer to her and she spread her legs wider to help him. Her skin was cold, her breathing growing faster. He moved slowly, his eyes on her, judging her expression. She felt his shaking fingers and suddenly pressure filled her as he slid inside. He didn't move right away, allowing her body to adjust to accommodate his size. It was strange, feeling him in the place that had always been empty.

"Are you okay?" he asked.

She nodded, a small whimper escaping her throat. He leaned down, kissing her neck as he began to move inside of her. The feeling was new, but amazing. She moved rhythmically with him, their bodies fitting together like they'd been made that way. Made for each other.

EIGHTEEN

GUNNER

July 2010

His tossing and turning seemed to be keeping her awake. "I'm going outside for a bit," he whispered to her. She nodded, half asleep.

"Everything okay?" she asked, yawning.

He kissed her head. "I just need some air. Everything's fine," he assured her, slipping on his pants and easing out the door. Gunner walked down the hall, his body still wired from being with her. He couldn't sleep, for fear he'd forget a single thing about their night. He took a glass from the counter, filling it with water and taking a sip.

He walked out onto the deck, shutting the door quietly and looking at the purple sky. The morning felt alive somehow, better. A permanent smile filled his all-too-often stony face.

He shook his head, still in disbelief. Reagan had changed

his world so much since she'd come into it. Not just in the obvious ways, but in small ways, too. He now found himself in a good mood more often. He had something to look forward to. She was his happy place, and he hadn't fully allowed himself to admit it until that night. He felt his wall starting to break for her.

He took another drink of water, running a hand through his hair and yawning. It was amazing how much he felt for her. Love, hope, protection, desire...it was all there, swirling and spinning inside of him. Before this, before Reagan, he'd never dreamed he could love someone the way he loved her. He would do anything for her. His heart jumped in his chest at just the thought of being with her.

He took another drink, pulling a cigarette from his pocket and lighting it. He had to be realistic. Reagan wouldn't love him for long. She couldn't. Soon enough, she'd see how damaged he was. She'd realize he wasn't right for her, wasn't enough for her, and he'd have to let her go. He would, though it would destroy him, because it was what she needed. Someone whole. Someone who could love her the way a girl like her should be loved. Gunner could never be that guy, though he had tried so hard. Truth was, there was a darkness inside him...a darkness that was always lurking in the back of his mind. He was meant to be alone. His greatest fear was hurting her, breaking her heart the way he'd watched his dad break his mom's every day. He was cruel to her. Cold. Distant. Gunner had never seen them smile at each other. Most days, they were hateful roommates, arguing over food or bills. And those were the good days, the ones that didn't end with an emergency room visit.

He could never let Reagan see that side of his life. He

hated that he'd even told her about it. He didn't want her pity or her worry. He wanted to take care of her, to be exactly what she wanted. Despite everything, every good intention he had for her, he spent every day waiting for her to tell him his time was up. She was going to move on—it was inevitable. Girls like Reagan Orrick didn't love guys like him. They couldn't. Not really, because they'd never truly know them. She'd never know Gunner the way she wanted, and therefore would never be able to love him the way she needed.

He heard a door shut inside the quiet house and then footsteps. A door shut again. Wondering if she'd woken up, he walked back inside. As he set the cup down in the sink, his eyes searched the dark room for her, but she was nowhere to be found. He tiptoed across the hardwood floors on his way to the bathroom. He grabbed the bottle of blue mouthwash from the sink, not wanting to rid himself of the taste of her but also not wanting to knock her out with his morning breath. He hadn't thought to bring a toothbrush, so the mouthwash would have to do. He walked to the toilet, lifting up the seat to relieve his full bladder. The water in the bowl was still running and he realized she must've woken up to use the restroom.

Suddenly, he heard quiet laughter, and then whispers coming from the bedroom. What the hell is she doing? *he wondered sleepily, a yawn overtaking him.*

He turned, pulling his pants back up, flushing the toilet, and running his hands under the water quickly. He exited the room, crossing the hall and twisting the bedroom doorknob. He walked into the bedroom, staring at her in the pale moonlight. Just like that, his whole world—every happiness in his life—shattered before his eyes.

NINETEEN

GUNNER

July 2010

Gunner pulled into the driveway at top speed, flinging gravel as he came to a stop. He jumped out of his car, running up the front walk and slamming the door as he entered the house.

His mother sat in her worn, green wingback chair. She frowned at him as he walked past her. "Is that how you enter my house?" she snapped at him angrily.

"Sorry," he said, barely casting a look her way. He stomped down the hall, slamming his bedroom door and grabbing a bag from his closet.

His bedroom door swung open a moment later and Gia stood there. Her cheek bore a long, purple bruise. "Gunner?" she asked, tears in her dark eyes. "Where are you going?"

He shoved the measly contents of his drawers into the bag. "What happened to you?" he asked, already knowing the answer.

"I'm fine," she dismissed him, her hand moving to her cheek for a second. "Where were you last night? Gavin never came home either." He didn't stop moving, filling his bag with anything he could grab. When she realized he wasn't going to answer, she went on. "You're leaving, aren't you?"

He nodded, looking at her finally. "It's time."

"Take me with you," she begged, more tears suddenly in her eyes.

He stopped then, approaching her and brushing a thumb over her bruised cheek. "I'm sorry, Gia, I can't."

"You can't leave us," she cried, panic filling her voice.

"I can't stay here anymore. I'm sorry. I know I promised you...but I can't. And I can't take you with me. You have school. I can't take care of you." He shook his head, stepping back and stuffing a few remaining things into the duffel bag.

"It'll get worse," she pleaded with him. "It'll all get worse without you here, Gun. You protect us. We're safe as long as you're here."

He slammed a drawer shut. "Safe? Gia, look at you. I'm not protecting you from anything. The only way I know to protect you is to go to the police. Do you want to do that? 'Cause I'll take you right now."

She lowered her head. "You know I can't."

"Then, what am I supposed to do? I'm not going to keep sitting around waiting for him to kill one of you."

"Maybe that wouldn't be the worst thing." He heard the weight in her voice as she said it. It wasn't something that had slipped off of her tongue in the heat of the moment, but rather something she'd put thought into.

"What are you talking about?"

"I'd rather die than keep living this way." Her voice was firm, her eyes swimming with tears.

"You don't mean that."

"I'm a prisoner, Gunner. Of course I do."

"You only have another year and you'll be free. Just one more year."

"Don't you see how screwed up we are? We will never be free."

"Gia, please don't talk like that. After you graduate, I'll be settled somewhere. Then you can come with me. I'll keep you safe."

"And Gavin?" she asked, her eyes filled with hope.

"Gavin can take care of himself," he said through gritted teeth.

"He's in as much danger as I am."

"Gavin would protect himself if it came down to it. He'd choose himself over you. Don't let him fool you."

"He's our brother," she said under her breath, taking obvious offence to his words.

"He's a self-righteous, selfish prick, Gia. Open your eyes," he yelled, anger bubbling over.

"Don't you yell at me," she snapped. "If you weren't so quick to judge him, maybe the two of you could get along. He's not so bad, Gun."

He huffed. "Fat chance."

"You guys let your big heads get in the way. You're brothers. And you need each other. But neither of you can see that."

"We don't," he said sharply. "We've never needed each other. And we never will. I don't have time to have this argument with you again."

"Please don't do this, Gunner. I need you." She pressed her hands together, as if in prayer, begging him to stay.

He rubbed his chin in frustration. "Fine. Pack a bag. Necessities only. We leave in fifteen minutes."

She shook her head, her eyes haunted. "I can't."

"What? You just said that's what you wanted."

"Not without him."

"You're choosing him?" he asked, pain filling his chest at her betrayal.

She nodded firmly. "I will always choose him. He's my brother."

"I thought I was too," he said, hurt in his voice as he stormed out of the room.

"Gunner, wait!" she yelled, chasing him through the house. "Please!"

Misty appeared in front of them, a frown on her wrinkled face. "What do you two think you're doing? What's with all the yelling? You're going to wake your daddy."

"I'm leaving, Momma," Gunner told her, his voice low.

"Leaving? What do you mean?"

"I'm out. Done. This is goodbye."

"Quit being dramatic. What's going on?" his mother asked, confusion on her face.

He took hold of her bony, frail shoulders and hugged her tight. "I'm leaving Dale," he said, "and I won't ever be back."

"You can't leave us," she said, her eyes wild with fear.

Behind them, Gia's sobs could be heard. "Please, Gunner," she begged.

"He'll kill us all," his mother warned. "If you leave, we're as good as dead."

"Then, come with me. We'll leave right now. By the time he notices, we'll be long gone."

"No," she silenced him, her voice quiet. "It won't work, Gun. Not like this."

"I won't stay another night in this town. Come with me or not, either way I'm leaving right now."

He waited for them to respond and when neither did, he hugged them both at once, a sob burning in the back of his throat. "I'll do whatever I can to take care of you, I promise," he said, though he wasn't sure how he could promise such a thing. "But I have to go."

"I love you," Gia said, kissing his cheek. "I understand," she whispered in his ear, "and I forgive you. This isn't your fault."

When she pulled away, she was broken, her eyes as empty as if he'd killed her himself. He took her face in his hands, kissing her head. "I'm going to take care of you. I promise I'll be back for you."

TWENTY

GUNNER
PRESENT DAY

Gunner walked out of the bedroom, his hair had been brushed and styled for the first time in months. He wore an old, button down shirt and the only jeans he owned without permanent stains. He tried to hide the excitement he felt—the foolish hope he'd sworn not to have.

"You look nice, Gun," his mom said, looking him over.

"Thanks."

"Will you be home tonight? Or should I not expect you?"

"I'll be home," he assured her. "It's just dinner."

She smiled slyly. "Well, I won't wait up."

He shrugged. "Have you seen my shoes?"

She pointed to the door. "Where you left them."

"Oh," he said, grabbing the worn boots and pulling them onto his feet.

"Do you have any plans tomorrow?" she asked, just as he

was exiting the house. He stepped back in, shutting the screen door.

"Not yet, why do you ask?"

"I go visit their graves on Wednesdays. I thought maybe you'd like to go with me."

He closed his eyes, rubbing his temples. "Not particularly, no," he told her.

"Gunner—"

"Let it go, Mom," he warned.

"I know you don't—"

"No, you don't. You don't know. I don't want to go. Why can't you just accept that?"

"I don't understand how you can be so heartless. You need to go. You didn't even come home for the funeral."

"You know why I didn't."

"They're your brother and sister, Gunner. You owe them more than this."

"I owe them nothing," he spat. "I don't have to go to their graves to grieve them. Everything I ever did was to protect them."

"Until it wasn't."

"Don't put that on me." His voice filled with venom.

She put her hands up in defeat. "I said I wasn't going to do this. I told myself if you ever decided to come home, I wasn't going to bring them up. I didn't want to upset you. But—"

"But you did anyway," he said angrily, walking out the door without another word. He climbed into the car, rage pulsing through him and drove to her house. *Her parents' house,* he reminded himself. The moment was filled with dèjá vu; he'd pulled up to this very spot so many times before, walked up to that same front door, waiting for the girl inside.

This time, when he knocked, the girl who answered was a miniature version of Reagan—the only difference being her jet black hair. Gunner's hair.

"Hello," she said, smiling politely. "Are you here to see my mom?"

He bent down so that he was eye level with her. "Yes, I am. You must be Nora." *My Nora. My daughter, Nora.* The girl was undeniably beautiful—her ivory skin the perfect compliment to her dark hair, freckles, and sea-green eyes.

"Yes, sir. You must be Gunner. My mom isn't ready yet."

Just then, as if on cue, a frazzled Reagan appeared from behind her. "Nora," she scolded, "what have I told you about answering the door?"

"But I knew it was your friend," the girl argued.

"It doesn't matter," Reagan said. "Remember the rules. Now, go back in the kitchen with Grandma and let Mommy talk for a moment."

"Fine." The girl pouted but obeyed, walking from the room.

"Goodbye, Nora," Gunner called after her, sad to see her go. Once she was out of sight, he looked up at Reagan. "You ready to go?"

She shook her head. "I'm sorry, Gunner. I'm going to have to cancel."

"What? Why?" he asked, disappointment filling him.

Tears brimmed her eyes. "I have no one to watch Nora. My parents just got a call. The police are releasing her body to us so Mom and Dad are flying up to New York tonight."

She was nearing her breaking point, it was all over her

face. “I’m so sorry, Rae,” he told her honestly. “Is there anything I can do?”

She shook her head. “I’m fine,” she said, though her voice cracked as she said it.

“Well, you obviously aren’t.”

“I will be,” she said, reading his doubtful expression. “Gunner, *I will be fine.* I just can’t go out tonight. I’m sorry.”

“What if we stayed in? I could help you with Nora, maybe get to know her a little bit better. You shouldn’t be alone.”

She scowled. “I’m good at being alone, Gunner, I’ve had a lot of practice. You made sure of that.” Her words were sharp but as she spoke again they carried a different tone. “And besides, I don’t know if that’s such a good idea.”

“You said yourself we need to talk. For Nora’s sake if nothing else. I’ll even cook you both dinner if you want.”

She raised her eyebrows. “You cook?”

He smiled. “I am a macaroni and cheese aficionado.”

She pressed her lips together, her forehead wrinkling in deep thought. “Nora only knows that you’re my old friend. You can’t tell her anything else.”

“I won’t tell her anything until you’re ready.”

“Okay,” she said hesitantly. “But this is just so we can talk. For Nora.”

“For Nora,” he agreed.

“And if I change my mind, you’ll leave.”

“Of course,” he vowed.

“Nora!” she called over her shoulder. “Get your stuff, baby.” She held up a finger. “I’ll be out in just a second. We can go back to my house.”

He nodded. “Okay, sure. I’m going to run to the store

and grab a few things." She shut the door, leaving him standing on the doorstep alone.

"MOM DOESN'T EAT MACARONI," Nora informed him, eyeing the box as he sat it on the counter.

"Well, that's just because she's never tried mine." He winked at her.

"She says it goes straight to her butt," she said, letting out a giggle.

"Nora!" her mother said, her face flushing.

"Well, you do," she insisted. "Hey, can I preheat the oven?" She changed the subject quickly, her eyes on Gunner. He looked to Reagan, awaiting a response though her question was directed to him. When she nodded, he handed Nora the bag of chicken nuggets.

"Three-fifty," he told her.

She hurried to the stove excitedly while Gunner grabbed a pot from the rack above the island. He filled it with water before handing it to Nora. "Can you sit this on the stove for me?"

Reagan walked to the fridge, grabbing a block of cheese and setting it down. "At least use real cheese, please, rather than that powdered poison." She smiled at him, her tone soft, though he could tell it was important to her. She was so different than the girl who'd scarfed pizza rolls and beef jerky with him so many years ago.

"When did your mom become such a food snob?" he teased Nora, tossing the powdered cheese packet in the trash.

Nora shrugged. "Did you know my mom in school?"

"I sure did," he told her, chopping up the cheese. She grabbed a baking sheet, placing the chicken nuggets onto it carefully. From across the room, Reagan stared at the bag, a worried look on her face. She wanted to protest, he could tell, but she was remaining quiet.

"Don't worry," he teased her, "they're organic, gluten-free, grass-fed, non-gmo, cage free, free range, and blessed by a gypsy spirit."

Reagan couldn't help but smile at him, though she turned away as he saw it.

"What was she like?" Nora asked.

"The chicken?" Gunner joked, poking a nugget. "I didn't know her personally, but I've heard she was a real pain."

Nora laughed, maybe a bit too loud. "No, I meant my mom when you were in school."

"Oh." Gunner feigned confusion. "She was," he looked up, meeting her eyes, "brilliant. Beautiful." He tapped the girl's nose. "Just like you. And smart. And funny. But she had a stubborn streak."

"She always says I'm stubborn, too."

"Well, you come by it naturally."

"See," Nora taunted her mother. "It's your fault." Reagan approached her, taking the baking sheet and sliding it into the oven.

"I'll take credit for that, 'cause I get credit for a lot of great stuff about you too," she said, kissing her daughter's head.

"Did you know my dad?" Nora asked.

"What?" Gunner asked, doing a double take at her

words. He popped a piece of cheese into his mouth to buy some time, staring at Reagan.

"My dad. Mom said he went to school with her, so you probably knew him too, right?"

Reagan shook her head. "I don't know if Gunner knew your dad or not, baby."

"Mom says I have his smile," she told him matter-of-factly.

"Well, I'm sure he was great."

"I never met him," she said. "He left when I was still in Mom's belly."

"I'll bet he wishes he could've met you," he said, tears burning his eyes. He looked away, inhaling sharply.

"Yeah, maybe. Jesse says he was strange."

"Jesse?" Gunner's heart skipped a beat. "Who's Jesse?"

"Mom's fiancé," the girl answered simply, grabbing a piece of cheese for herself. "I think he'll be my dad after they get married, right, Mom?" She smiled proudly.

Reagan nodded, though her eyes were on Gunner. "Hey, Nor, why don't you go wash up for supper, okay?"

"Okay." The girl disappeared down the hall, humming to herself.

Reagan looked to Gunner. "I didn't want you to find out that way. I wasn't hiding it...I just wanted to wait and tell you when we could really talk."

He held up his hand. "You don't owe me an explanation, Rae. You're allowed to have a life. I would be lying if I said I'm surprised. I'm here for Nora, remember? I'm not delusional enough to believe we were just going to fall back into what we were."

"I know, I just...I didn't want you to find out from anyone else."

"Well, I'm glad I know," he lied.

"You are?"

"I'm glad you're happy." Well, at least that part was true.

"Thank you," she said as Nora appeared back in the room and the macaroni began to boil over.

AN HOUR LATER, Gunner was clearing the table. He carried a pile of dishes to the sink just as Reagan appeared from down the hall.

"She's down for the night. Oh, you don't have to clean those," she told him as he threw a towel over his shoulder and flipped the faucet on.

"It's no problem," he assured her, adding a bit of soap to the water. She walked over to stand beside him, her back resting against the counter, watching him work. The water scalded his hands, though he could focus on nothing but her as he rolled his sleeves up and began scrubbing.

"You were good with her tonight," she said, surprising him.

"I was?"

"Yeah. You impressed me."

He shrugged. "She's an awesome kid."

"So," she began, "elephant in the room."

"Yeah?" Dread filled him immediately as he tried to read her expression.

"I mean, hi, how are you...haven't seen you since you took my virginity and left town without a word."

He frowned. "You know why I left, Reagan."

"I know why you *think* you left."

He turned off the water, shaking his head. "I couldn't face you. I didn't want to hate you."

"Gunner, it wasn't what you thought."

"Really?" he asked harshly. "Because it sure as hell looked like—" He stopped himself. "I don't want to fight with you."

She touched his arm gently, his body on high alert. "You need to know the truth."

He stepped back. "No. I don't. I can't. You deserved him, Rae. I always said you deserved a guy like Gavin. I just never thought you would actually fall for him. I was stupid enough to believe you really cared about me. I never thought you would sleep with my brother." He felt his face growing more red by the minute.

"I didn't sleep with Gavin," she insisted. "I wouldn't. You've got it all wrong."

TWENTY-ONE

REAGAN

July 2010

Reagan dreamed of Gunner's body surrounding hers. She smiled, though she somehow knew it was a dream. A door shut somewhere in the distance, rousing her from sleep. He was still missing. She ran her hands over his empty side of the bed, sitting up.

"Where'd you go?" she asked, hearing his feet sliding over the carpet lazily. He didn't answer. In the pitch black room, she tried hard to make out his silhouette. She felt the covers lifting, his body sliding into the bed with her once again. He wrapped his arms around her, his lips on hers. She welcomed his kiss, laying back on the pillow. He rolled over on top of her and she let out a quiet laugh. He was already hard against her leg.

"I guess this means you're ready for round two," she whispered, his breath on her neck. She ran her hands over his bare

chest, in her half-asleep state she realized she had never noticed how defined it felt. She'd been so nervous before, she hadn't taken the time to enjoy him.

She felt him slide inside of her suddenly, her soreness evident, and she let out a whimper. "Easy," she begged.

"You feel amazing," he told her, his lips on her ear.

His voice sounded strange and, more awake now, she realized there was alcohol on his breath.

She tensed. "Hey, have you been—" On the other side of the room, she heard the door open and someone was standing in the doorway. She pulled the covers up to shield them from the intruder. The light flipped on, burning her eyes and she covered them instinctively. When she opened them, she stared at Gunner, the heartbreak and betrayal written all over his face. Her eyes traveled to the man on top of her, still not completely comprehending what was happening, and gasped. Gavin's expression was just as shocked.

"What the—" he said, jumping off of her and covering up with the sheet.

She looked to the door. "Gunner!" she cried, crawling out of bed and looking for her clothes. Her whole body shook as she searched. "I'm so sorry," she said, sounding completely pathetic even to herself. "This isn't what it looks like." She pulled her shirt over her head, not bothering with a bra. When she looked to the doorway to try to explain, he was gone.

"Reagan, I'm—" Gavin began to speak but she couldn't listen, couldn't bear to look him in the eye. She pulled on her pants as she ran from the door, her heart pounding as loud as her footsteps on the hardwood.

"Gunner, please!" she screamed, running through the dark house. She heard his car door slam and the engine started

up. He peeled out of the driveway before she'd made it to the door. She fell to her knees on the wooden porch, tears pouring down her face in all-out sobs. "Please...come...back," she cried out, physical pain filling her chest.

She couldn't believe she had been so stupid; she'd known it wasn't Gunner. She had to have. Everything about the brothers was different: the way they felt, the way they smelled, they way they held her. She pressed her palms onto her eyes, trying to calm the hysterical cries that were escaping her throat. Bile rose into her mouth and she stood, barely making it to the edge of the porch before her stomach began emptying.

She cursed through the vomit, rubbing her stomach in pain. She felt completely empty. It was as if a Gunner-sized hole had been ripped through her insides. She felt hands on her back and the feral sobs calmed slightly as she saw her sister.

"Rae?" Holly asked, her voice small. She had tears in her own eyes.

"Get Gavin's keys," Reagan instructed, snot and tears were coating her face, but she couldn't be bothered to clean it.

Holly remained still, looking frightened. "What happened? Gavin's panicking."

"Get the damn keys, Holly!" she screamed at her sister, who retreated without a word. When she returned a few moments later, Gavin wasn't with her. It was a good thing, Reagan thought, given that she was ready to claw his throat out with her bare hands. Holly handed over her phone and bag, helping her sister to the car. Reagan dialed Gunner's number, listening to it ring and ring.

"Hey, it's Gunner. Leave me a message," the voicemail played.

"Gunner," she cried, cradling the phone. "Please, please, please call me back. Please. I'm so sorry. I thought it was you, Gun. I thought he was you. I love you. Please call me back. Please." She cried louder as she hung up and Holly began pulling the truck down the long driveway.

"Reagan, what happened?" she asked again. Reagan's gaze left the phone.

"I have to find him," Reagan whispered incessantly, her eyes wild. "I have to talk to him. He needs to understand. He'll never forgive me. I'm such an idiot." She rambled on, thoughts pouring from her crazed mind.

Holly touched her sister's arm. "Did he...did Gavin rape you?" she asked, her voice shaking with obvious dread.

Reagan thought about the question. They'd been having sex, sort of. And it wasn't what she wanted. But, judging by the look on his face, it wasn't what he had wanted either. He was drunk. It was a mistake from what she could tell. "No, I don't think so."

"Did he cheat on me?" she asked, the tears on her cheeks showing a breakable side of her sister Reagan rarely saw.

Reagan tried to reassure her, fill her with a sense of peace that she couldn't find in herself. "No, Hol, I don't think he did. It was dark. He was drunk. When Gunner flipped on the light, Gavin looked just as shocked as the rest of us. I think he was looking for you."

"He drank way too much," Holly agreed. Her sister's reassurance seemed to have calmed her. "Are you going to be okay?"

"No," Reagan told her honestly. "I just need to see Gunner. He's never going to forgive me."

"It was an accident," Holly said, wiping her own tears. "He loves you. He'll forgive you once he understands."

"No," Reagan argued. "You don't get it. Gavin is like...his weakness. I don't know if there's any coming back from this. Even if he forgives me, I don't think he'll ever look at me the same. Oh, Holly, what am I going to do? I can't live without him."

Holly placed her hand on the back of Reagan's head, rubbing her hair gently. "We'll make sure you don't have to," she promised. "You two are going to be okay."

Reagan couldn't even muster a smile, her body feeling bruised as if she wore her broken heart on the outside. "I love him so much, Holly. I've never felt this way about anyone. I can't lose him."

"You won't," her sister said, making a promise they both knew couldn't be kept.

WHEN THE GIRLS *pulled into Dale, Reagan was ready to jump out of her seat. As they turned into the driveway of Gunner's home, the one he'd never let her visit, her stomach began to churn. What would he have told his family? Would they all hate her? When the truck stopped, she climbed out quickly, looking around for his car. It wasn't there.*

The front door of the house opened and Gia appeared, obviously surprised to see her there with Gavin's truck and no Gavin.

"What happened?" Gia asked. "Where's my brother?"

"He's...we borrowed his truck." She didn't have time to explain. "Is Gunner home?"

She shook her head, stepping out onto the porch and shutting the door. "What did you do, Reagan?" she demanded. It was the first time she had heard Gia's voice sound anything but meek.

"I just need to see him. It's a long story."

"He's gone," Gia told her, glancing toward the driveway. Reagan noticed a bruise on her cheek she hadn't seen at first.

"Are you okay?" she asked.

"I'm fine," Gia said, touching her face. "But you should go."

"Do you know where he might have gone?" Reagan went on.

"He's gone," she repeated. "As in forever."

The words hit her square in the chest, physically causing her to take a step back. "W-what?" She blinked back the tears that had been stinging her eyes.

"I'm sorry," Gia said, though she didn't really look it. "I don't know what happened between you two, but he is gone. And I don't think either of us will ever see him again."

"Who's there?" a woman's voice called from inside the house, causing Gia to flinch.

"You should go," she said again, opening the door. "And please don't come here again." With that, she disappeared into the house, leaving Reagan to stumble back to the truck of the boy who had ruined it all.

TWENTY-TWO

REAGAN

July 2010

It was just before six the next morning and Reagan hadn't slept a wink. She sat on the end of her bed, tears still falling. Her body was sore—from her night with him, from sobbing for hours on end, and from the lack of food and sleep. She felt like she couldn't move, paralyzed by the fear of never seeing the boy who held her heart again.

She checked her phone for the one hundredth time, staring at the picture of the two of them that sat on her wallpaper. No calls. No texts. Nothing. He'd shut his phone off after a few hours but she continued to call, finding small comfort in being able to hear his voice on the voicemail.

A quiet knock sounded on her bedroom door, but she didn't respond. Couldn't. When the door opened, her eyes didn't bother moving to see who had walked in. It wasn't him, so it didn't matter.

Holly sat down beside of her carefully, moving a piece of hair back toward her ponytail. "Reagan?" Reagan heard the tears in her voice, breaking her trance. She looked at her sister, noticing the bright red eyes and splotchy skin.

"What is it?" she asked. It was the first time she'd heard her own voice all day. Holly sucked in a breath, her chin quivering and Reagan knew what was coming. Gunner was dead. *The tears began to fall harder but she managed to maintain her composure. She waited for the blow.*

Holly breathed out slowly, preparing them both. She wiped the tears as quickly as they fell. "Something happened," she whispered.

"He's dead, isn't he?" Reagan asked, the calm in her voice surprising her.

"Gavin."

"Gavin?" The name caused her stomach to knot up. "What did he do?" She spoke through gritted teeth.

"Gavin's dead," Holly said.

"What?" She wasn't sure if she instantly filled with relief or shock.

"There was a fire. Momma just got a call. They're...they're all dead. Gavin...Gia...their dad. Their mother is in the hospital." She was sobbing, her words coming out in short bursts. Nothing seemed to make sense to Reagan, her sister's words all mashing together in her brain.

"What?" she asked, because no response she could think of made any sense.

"He's just...gone." Holly fell into her lap, shaking. Reagan stroked her hair calmly.

"Gunner wasn't there?" she asked. She knew it was selfish, but it was the only thing that seemed to be on her mind.

Holly's head shook with a firm no, tears continuing to fall. Reagan continued to run her fingers through her sister's hair, wiping her own tears occasionally. They were a strange sight —two sisters, broken by brothers who were nothing but broken themselves.

"Hol?" Reagan asked, her voice shaking.

"Yeah?" she asked.

"Nothing. Nevermind," she said, unable to ask the question that was on her mind. It wasn't possible. He'd been angry, sure. Furious with her and Gavin both. But he wouldn't. Couldn't. She knew him and she knew he wasn't capable of it. And yet, the question remained, floating around her mind: had Gunner done this?

TWENTY-THREE

GUNNER

Present Day

Gunner stared at her, the room was eerily still around them. He couldn't believe what he'd just heard.

"You weren't cheating on me with Gavin?"

"Of course not, Gunner. Of course I wasn't. It was an accident on both of our parts. He was just...drunk. And I was half asleep. I thought it was you climbing into bed. With the room so dark, I couldn't tell. I know that sounds like a lame excuse, but I swear to you I didn't know." He turned away from her, pacing the room angrily. "I tried to tell you. I tried to call, to find you...but I couldn't. I had no idea where you'd gone or when, *if*, you'd be back. You have no idea how much I struggled after you left. I realize you were angry, but I can't understand how you could just walk away like you did without even hearing me out."

He looked up at her, stopping in his tracks. "You can't

understand?" His eyes grew soft. "Rae, do you understand the power you had over me? Do you understand that my heart, my soul, everything...I gave it to you. All that time, you fought for me to let my wall down for you, but the truth was...my wall crumbled for you before I ever had the chance to stop it. I fell for you harder than I even knew possible. Everything I did, every breath I took...was for you. And when I saw you two together, after all the times I worried about you wanting someone like him...it destroyed me. From the inside out. The days after I left, months, years...I was broken. I was miserable, empty...I left a part of myself here with you. And I'll never get that back. I couldn't stay and watch you love my brother. It would've killed me. And, once I was gone, I stayed gone because I wanted you to be happy. Above all, that was, *is,* what matters to me. Seeing you together made me realize you deserve someone better than me. Someone who could do better for you. I'd always believed that. But, if I'd known the truth, and if I'd known about Nora, I wouldn't have left. Of course I wouldn't have. I couldn't." From across the room, he could see the tears in her eyes. "I'm so sorry, Reagan. I know I could say that every day for the rest of my life and it wouldn't make it okay, but you don't know how sorry I am."

She lowered her head, completely silent. He saw her shoulders begin to shake as sobs overtook her. He rushed to her side, his hands on her back as he tried to console her. Tears filled his own eyes as he watched her break down and knew he was to blame. She gave in, letting herself fall into his arms, her fists on his chest. He patted her hair carefully, whispering in her ear. His lips kissed the top of her head without conscious thought. "I'm so sorry," he repeated.

After a few moments, her crying seemed to slow and she pulled away. "I wish that was enough," she whispered. "You left me here."

"I know."

"You broke my heart."

"I never meant to."

"That doesn't matter, Gunner. It still happened. It still hurt. And I blamed myself, I still do sometimes, even though I know I didn't purposefully do anything wrong."

"It's like you said...in the end it still hurts all the same, purposefully or not. I know I broke your heart, but I've spent eight years trying to heal mine, too."

She nodded. "I know. It wasn't really your fault, and it wasn't really mine. But, at the same time, we're both to blame."

"All that matters now is that we know the truth."

"There is one thing I still don't know about."

"What's that?"

She bit her lip nervously, her eyes searching his. "Don't hate me for asking."

"Just tell me."

"Did you have something to do with their deaths?" she asked, her eyes closed.

His jaw dropped and he tried not to hesitate. "*What?* No! Of course not."

She let out a sigh of relief and her face said she believed him. "I didn't want to think so, but it was strange timing. I had to ask."

"You brought me home to Nora without knowing the answer to that question?"

"I knew you weren't a danger to us, Gun."

"How could you possibly know that? It's been eight years...a lot has changed since I last saw you."

"That may be true, but I never doubted how much you loved me. And, if you loved me like I loved you...you'd sooner die than harm me. Or Nora."

He swallowed hard as she said it. *Loved.* Past-tense. As in, she didn't love him anymore. Hadn't in a long time, most likely. "Right," he said, trying to seem as though he hadn't felt jilted by her comment. "Well, it was a long time ago. We were just dumb kids. You're with someone new now, so we need to focus on Nora and what we can do to make this easy on her. I want to make sure I'm a part of her life." His words were harsher than he'd meant them to be and she took a step back.

"Have you changed your mind about staying?"

"No," he said, "I still need to go back to New York eventually. My life is there now. But Nora could come stay with me for the summer, maybe. We could work out something where we rotate holidays...or whatever you think would be best."

"If you think, for one minute, I'm going to let you take my daughter to the same city where my baby sister was just murdered, you're insane."

"*Our* daughter," he reminded her. "And I would never let anything happen to her."

"You can't promise that. No. I'm sorry, but if you want to see Nora, you'll have to come home."

"This isn't my home anymore," he said, hitting his hand on the island, suddenly angry.

"It's hers." Reagan was standing her ground. He knew that stubborn look in her eyes all too well. "I'm sorry,

Gunner. I'm not trying to be unreasonable. I'm really not. I know you want to see her and I appreciate that. But New York is non-negotiable. And if you try to fight me...well, as far as any court is concerned, you abandoned her before she was born."

Her words stung and he wanted to argue but decided against it. "I would never try to take her from you. You're her mother, Rae. She needs you." He took a deep breath, thinking. "I'll just have to make trips back to Dale more often. I can make it work. I just wish I could see her more than I'll be able to."

"Why are you in New York anyway? What took you there?"

He shrugged. "It was far away from here."

She walked to the refrigerator and placed the container full of leftovers into it. "And do you like it? Are you happy there?"

"That's a loaded question," he said with a smirk, "but yeah. It's all right."

"What do you do?" She sat down at the island, her face in her hands as if she were hearing the most interesting thing in the world.

"It's called biomedical decon. But most people just call me a cleaner." He watched her expression change from interest to confusion.

"A cleaner? What are we talking about...like a housekeeper or the mob?"

He laughed loudly, starting to feel at ease with her again. They fit easily back into each other's lives, which made it all the more difficult for Gunner to keep his distance. "Neither. I clean crime scenes."

"Like dead bodies?" She looked mortified.

"Well, the bodies are usually gone before I arrive. I just clean up their mess."

She smiled, looking away as if she were thinking. "A cleaner, hm? How fitting for you. You always were cleaning up my messes."

"You weren't a mess."

"Is it disgusting?" she asked. It was one of the many questions Gunner hated answering. In short, of course it was. But that wasn't the answer people wanted to hear. At least, it wasn't the only answer. They wanted to hear details and Gunner couldn't get into them. Not here. Not with her. So, he settled on a vague answer.

"You get used to it after a while. But, yeah, most of the time it's pretty disgusting. What about you? What do you do?"

"I'm a teacher," she said.

"A teacher? That's perfect for you."

"I love it." Her smile told him she truly did.

"I'm glad you do. You're a good influence. Always have been."

"Did you wonder about me?" she asked, her voice cracking. He saw her then, not the confident woman who sat in front of him, but the terrified teenager he'd fallen so in love with.

"Every single day." His eyes locked with hers. They were both shocked by his brutal honesty.

She covered her eyes, concealing tears. "You shouldn't have left."

"I know," he said, taking her hands from her face and holding them gently. "But we can't change it now."

Her chin quivered. "I wish we could."

"No, you don't. Your life is beautiful, Rae. What you've done with Nora, this house, your job...everything is just the way you wanted. I'm proud of you."

"Nora grounded me. She kept me strong because I had to be for her. But that doesn't mean it was easy. I still waited for your call for months. I knew you weren't going to be the person knocking on my door or the one walking into the room but that didn't stop me from looking for you every single time. I searched for your car in every parking lot I pulled into. For years, Gunner. For years, I waited for you to come home to me. Nothing is how I wanted it to be."

"If I could change it, I would take it back in a heartbeat."

She took her hands back from his, wiping away a tear. "But you can't. No matter how bad we wish you could. Life goes on, right? It has to. And I'm really happy with Jesse. I am. He's good to me. To Nora."

"I'm glad he makes you happy," he said, taking a step away from her.

"It was supposed to be you," she said, looking up at him from behind her dark, tear-coated lashes. "But I don't know how to fix that now. There's just...too much missing."

"I know," he said, though he disagreed. "We're going to have to figure this all out as we go. But, I don't want you to feel bad about your living your life. You had every right to move on and find happiness. As long as you have that with Jesse, I'm fine."

"Did you...move on?" she asked, her voice hesitant. "Are you seeing someone?" He saw her glance to his hand, checking for a ring.

"No," he assured her. "Not right now. But, you know me...I do better alone."

She smiled half-heartedly. "I'm sorry, Gunner. I really am."

"I am too." He wasn't sure exactly what they were apologizing for.

TWENTY-FOUR

GUNNER

The day of Holly's funeral came too soon. Gunner arrived at the funeral home with his mother shortly after the visitation started. He'd bought a new suit, since the only other one he owned was the one he'd worn to prom. He laid eyes on Reagan immediately. She stood at the front of the room, near the casket. It was strange—something about her grief made her even more beautiful. Because she had experienced such immense pain, she was suddenly more real to him. More attainable. Suddenly, she wasn't something off in the distance to be admired, but rather a real person he could get close to. A real person he could love. A real person who might've once loved him back.

Nora stood beside her. She was too young to be feeling such grief. Gunner wanted nothing more than to go to her, stand beside them both and help them through something he knew so well. Death was comfortable to him. Familiar. Grief no longer felt foreign and cold. It was something he knew he could handle. Something he knew he was good at.

Interrupting his thoughts, he locked eyes with Reagan, who offered a small smile. He smiled back, lowering his head slightly as a sign of respect. A man approached her and she broke Gunner's eye contact. He could see only the back of the man's head, his blond hair slicked over. Gunner watched him kiss Reagan's lips and white-hot jealousy filled his belly.

The man turned around to stand beside her, his arm wrapping around her waist, his other hand on Nora's shoulder. Gunner's jaw dropped as he recognized him immediately. "Jesse" was Jesse Mathis, captain of the football team, son of the mayor. He was everything Gunner wasn't. Gunner closed his fists, pulling his mother's arm gently to direct her toward the line that had begun forming.

They made their way toward the casket fairly quickly. Gunner looked down at Holly's body, touching her hand gently and closing his eyes for a moment of silence. He tried to block out the images floating through his mind of the day he found her. When he opened his eyes, he looked her over once more. Her black hair was curled carefully around her face and her green dress perfectly matched her sister's eyes. Gunner looked away. Reagan was everywhere in his mind. No matter how hard he tried, he couldn't stop seeing her.

The pain of seeing Reagan again was like a sunburn you hadn't realized you'd gotten—you may be oblivious to it for a while, but eventually you're bound to scratch it and then it becomes all you can focus on. Reagan was his sunburn, but rather than fading with time, she burned more each day. New York had been a welcome distraction, but back in Dale he was a seventeen-year-old kid again...head over heels in love with the girl he knew he couldn't keep.

Staring at the two of them—Reagan and Jesse—a picture-perfect couple, he realized that he would have to leave Dale soon. That night, if possible. He couldn't take watching her love someone else. It would destroy him, just like it had before.

As the line moved, they made it to the family, quickly whispering their condolences to Gemma and Scott. Gemma smiled at him warmly, despite her tears. "I'm glad you could come, Gunner."

"I'm so sorry for your loss," came his automatic response. "This is my mother, Misty."

"I've always wanted to meet you," Gemma said politely. "Thank you both for coming."

When they reached Reagan, Jesse, and Nora, Jesse held out his hand. "Gunner, it's great to see you, man. I'm glad you could make it home."

"Thanks," Gunner said, shaking his hand firmly. "I'm glad I could, too." He looked to Reagan. "I'm really sorry."

"Thank you, Gunner."

Gunner leaned down to Nora, whose face was shiny with fresh tears. "Hey, kiddo. You hanging in there?"

Nora nodded. "I'm just really sad."

"I know," he told her, rubbing her head. "I am too."

THE NEXT DAY, Gunner drove through Dale on his way to her house. He couldn't leave without saying goodbye this time, no matter how badly he wanted to. He pulled up in front of the yellow house and walked up to the door, knocking.

Reagan answered the door after a few moments, looking like she'd just woken up.

"Gunner? What are you doing here?" She shielded her eyes from the sun.

"I came to say goodbye," he told her firmly.

"Goodbye? What do you mean? You're leaving already?"

"I am. I have to get back to work. My plan was to only stay for the funeral. I owed you both that."

"What about Nora?"

"I'll be back in a month or two. I won't stay gone for long anymore, I promise."

She shook her head, crossing her arms. "That's not enough, Gunner," she said, stepping further toward him and closing the door slightly.

"What would you rather I do?" He stood his ground, staring at her with doubt.

"I'd rather you stay here and be a father," she retorted.

"I can't just stay here, Rae. It isn't that simple. I have a life in New York. There's nothing here for me."

She rolled her eyes. "Whatever, Gunner. Whatever you say. Like always."

"Are you mad at me? I'm doing everything I know to do for you both, I really am."

"I'm not mad," she said angrily.

"Well, you're acting mad and I'm sorry, but you have no right to be. You're marrying Jesse, right?"

"Yes."

"Okay, then. I don't want to get in the way of that. But I'm also not going to sit around and watch you love him."

"You left me, Gunner. And it's not like you want me anymore, anyway. You said it yourself: we have to move on."

"Yes, have to. As in, still haven't. You know I haven't. And I won't as long as I'm still here...still seeing you. Which is why I have to leave."

She looked down, kicking a rock on the concrete. "What if I don't want you to leave?"

"Why wouldn't you?" he demanded.

"You know why."

"I don't, Reagan. Because you're with someone else. And that's fine, but I can't stay here and watch it happen." His tone grew serious as he spoke again. "It's breaking my heart." It was his last attempt at getting her back. "Can't you see that?"

Tears filled her eyes at his words. "I don't know what to do."

He stepped forward, brushing the tears away and lowering his voice. "I don't want to make your life more complicated. That wasn't my goal when I came home."

Suddenly, the door opened wider and Nora was standing in front of him. "What's going on?"

"Nothing, Nor," Reagan assured her. She wiped her tears quickly, stepping away from Gunner and touching the girl's shoulder. "Gunner just stopped by to tell us he's heading back home."

"You're leaving?" the girl asked, seemingly upset by the news.

"He can't stay, baby," she told her, her eyes on Gunner.

"But why?" Nora whined. "I like you."

"I like you too," Gunner said, bending down so he was

eye level to her. "I'll be back soon so we can get to know each other more."

"Jesse doesn't like you," she said matter-of-factly, eyeing him.

"Nora," Reagan scolded her. "Don't be rude. Why on earth would you say that?" She bent down to meet her eyes as well.

"That's what he said. He said Gunner was mean to you and he didn't think it was a good idea for him to be here."

"When did he say that?"

The girl looked down guiltily. "I heard you talking last night when you thought I was asleep."

"You know you aren't supposed to eavesdrop on our conversations." Her face grew tight with frustration.

"'Cause I might hear something bad?" she asked carefully.

"You might hear something meant for adult ears," Reagan confirmed.

"Mommy, does Jesse lie?" the girl asked, looking down, her voice innocent and small.

"Of course not, baby. Why?"

"So Gunner did hurt you?"

Reagan looked to Gunner before she answered. "Would you please come inside?" He followed her lead into the living room where Reagan sat Nora down on the couch and squatted in front of her, clutching the girl's knees. With a sigh, Reagan began to speak. "Gunner was a very good friend of Mommy's when we were in school."

"Like a Jesse friend or an Aunt Holly friend?"

Reagan winced at her sister's name, still raw from her loss. "Like a Jesse friend."

"You loved her?" she asked, her eyes lighting up as she looked at Gunner.

Before he could be stopped, the answer fell from his mouth. "Yes, I did." He smiled at her before looking to Reagan. Their eyes locked on one another. "Once upon a time, we were very in love."

"So did you hurt her?" Nora asked again, causing them to break eye contact.

"It's complicated," Reagan whispered, her words carefully chosen.

"But you said Jesse isn't a liar. So, if he isn't a liar, then he told the truth. He said Gunner hurt you."

Reagan patted her chest. "He did hurt my heart." She wiped a quick tear from the corner of her eyes. "But he didn't mean to. Gunner is a good friend to Mommy and it's okay now." Nora was quiet for a moment. "Do you understand, Nor?"

"Did Jesse tell the truth about everything?" Suddenly, there were tears in the little girl's eyes and Gunner began to panic. Reagan moved her hand to Nora's cheek swiftly, stroking her face.

"What else did you hear?"

Nora's bottom lip quivered as she looked between them, avoiding eye contact.

"Nora?" Reagan begged. "What is it, sweetie?" Nora's gaze fell to the floor. She swung her feet, bumping the bottom of the couch repeatedly. Reagan put up a hand to stop her. "Nora...tell me."

The girl looked to Gunner, tears continuing to fall from her wide eyes. "Are you my dad?"

The room was instantly silent. Gunner's stomach

twisted into a solid knot. His skin grew cold and a thin layer of sweat began collecting on his forehead. "Nora, I...I'm..."

"You said Jesse isn't a liar. And you also said two people have to be in love to have a baby. And you were in love. So, is he my dad?" she demanded, looking at Reagan.

"Yes," Reagan answered firmly and Gunner felt the weight of their secret leave his shoulders immediately.

"You are?" she asked, her voice rising.

"I am," he confirmed.

"Why didn't you want me, then?" she asked, her chin quivering again. She lifted her hands to cover her eyes.

Reagan pulled her into her arms, rubbing her back. "Oh, sweetheart, he did. It's really complicated. Gunner didn't know about you because he left and we didn't get to talk for a really long time."

"Didn't you want me to have a dad?" she asked.

"More than anything, Nor. I want that more than anything. That's why I was so happy you and Jesse get along so well."

"So, when you marry him...he'll be my daddy, right? Does that mean Gunner won't be anymore?"

Reagan covered her eyes, pinching the bridge of her nose. Gunner could see the stress in her temples. "Sweetheart, you are so loved. You know that, right?"

"Yes, I know."

"Okay, so there are plenty of people who love you. Mommy loves you and Grandma and Grandpa love you. And Aunt Holly loved you very much. And Jesse loves you and Gunner loves you, too. So, things are going to be a little different around here for a while, because Mommy and Jesse and Gunner have a lot to figure out. But, no matter what happens, you have to remember how much you are loved. That's the most important thing, okay?"

She frowned. "Okay."

"I know you have a lot of questions for us. And we'll try to answer them. We may not have the answers though...not yet."

"Okay," the girl repeated.

"So do you have anything you want to ask us right now?"

"Yes," she said softly.

"Okay, go ahead."

"Why do you have to leave?" she asked Gunner. Her eyes burned into his. Gunner swallowed hard, trying to find the words to speak.

"I don't," he said finally, the only words he could muster.

Reagan's head jerked to look at him in shock. "You're staying?"

He wasn't sure, but he couldn't possibly bring himself to break that little girl's heart. "I would love to stay." He smiled at her, soaking up her growing smile. "I do have to go home, though. At least for a little while." He watched her smile disappear. "I have to find a subletter for my apartment, pack up my stuff, and put in some notice at work. It'll take me a bit to find work and a place here."

"You're really staying?" Reagan asked doubtfully.

"I'm going to do everything in my power to make that happen."

"How long will you be gone?"

"I honestly don't know," he told her. "Not long, I hope."

"I don't want you to leave," Nora pouted dramatically. "You've already missed seven whole years of my life."

"Nora, I promise you I won't be gone long. We can talk

on the phone every day. We're going to get to know each other. That's a promise, too. I am sorry I've missed so much but I'll tell you what...I am really excited to be your dad."

She smiled. "So, can I go with you?"

"No," he said quickly. "No, you have to stay here with your mommy."

"But why?" she whined. "You said you're coming back, so why can't I go with you? Mom could go, too."

"Your mom needs you here," he said, looking to Reagan for help. She had a strange look on her face. "What?" he asked.

"We could go," she said, her eyes searching his.

"You said no to New York."

"I said no to *Nora* going to New York. But, if you really plan to come back...we could go with you."

"Are you serious?" He couldn't believe it, though he desperately wanted to.

"You and Nora need to spend more time together. You could show her where you live. We could help you pack up or whatever. I mean, we couldn't stay for long. But, we're on summer break from school, so it's not like we're busy with anything. Plus, it would give us time to really get this whole co-parenting situation figured out."

"What would Jesse think?" he asked, trying to conceal his smile.

"He knows it's important to me that the two of you have a relationship. Besides, he's away at a medical conference in Chicago for the next ten days. I could have him fly out to New York to pick us up after, if you still need to stay."

"Okay," he agreed. "If you're sure."

"Okay?" Nora squealed, hopping off the couch.

"If you're sure you can stand to spend that much time with me."

She flung her arms around his waist, nearly knocking him over.

"Go pack your bags, Nora. I'll be in there in a second to help you," Reagan instructed. When she was out of earshot, Reagan turned to Gunner. "Are you sure this is okay? I know I put you on the spot."

"I'll never say no to spending time with you. Either of you. But I'm not going to assure you this is a good idea."

"Why?"

"Because of who we are, Reagan. And because of who we were."

"What? Are you afraid you won't be able to keep your hands off of me?" she teased.

"Terrified," he admitted, his voice a low growl. Her eyes grew wide, the smile disappearing from her face. He felt his skin grow hot as her blank stare transformed into an innocent expression he'd once known well. Her lips parted slightly and her cheeks flushed.

"Gunner, I—"

He leaned in without meaning to. "Shhh," he quieted her, touching a thumb to her bottom lip. He tucked a piece of hair behind her ear, her skin familiar under his palms. She was close to giving in, he could see it in the way she was looking at him.

Her phone rang loudly, causing them to jump. Gunner backed away as she pulled it from her pocket.

"Hello?" she called into the phone, her eyes still on him. "Mom, hey, I was just getting ready to call you...what's wrong?" Her eyes grew wide and she covered her exposed ear though he was making no noise. He watched her disappear down the hallway.

After a few moments, she returned. She was ghastly white, her mouth slumped open.

"What's wrong?" he asked.

"It's about Holly," she stammered, looking as though she may pass out.

"What about her? Did they figure something out?"

She nodded, a haunted expression on her face.

"What is it, Rae?" he asked, almost afraid to know.

"The results of her toxicology report came back. They're ruling it a heroin overdose."

"What?" His insides twisted at her words. "Was she on drugs?"

"I don't think so," she cried. "I mean, she was always a partier, but I never saw her do anything harder than pot. Then again, I had no idea she was living in New York so I guess I didn't know her as well as I thought."

"I'm so sorry, Reagan."

"That's not all, Gunner," she said, holding her hand up to stop him as he walked closer.

"What do you mean?" He froze.

"Something else showed up on her results."

"Another drug?"

"No," she said, her breathing growing faster. "Holly was pregnant."

TWENTY-FIVE

GUNNER

When they pulled up to the hotel near Louisville, Gunner looked in the backseat. Nora was sound asleep, her face pressed against the window. Reagan smiled at him, touching his shoulder. When they'd stopped, she'd been nearing sleep herself.

"You can go ahead and check us in. I'll grab her."

He nodded, following instructions. As he walked into the lobby, a slightly nicer place than he would've stayed at alone, he glanced around before walking to the front desk. "I need to check in."

"Okay," the man behind the counter said politely. "Just one?"

"There are three of us. We'll need two beds." Gunner pulled out his wallet.

"Are you a rewards member?" the man asked, staring at the computer screen.

"No."

"Oh," he held out the word, wincing. "Unfortunately, all we have left are king beds." Gunner frowned, looking back to the parking lot and trying to make a decision. "You could book two separate rooms, though." Gunner wasn't sure if he was being taken advantage of, but he didn't have time to waste. "Okay, fine. Two rooms."

"Very well." The man took the card from Gunner's hand and charged the rooms, handing over two room keys. "I was able to get you adjoining rooms, hopefully that will help."

"Thanks," he said softly, watching as Reagan entered the building carrying Nora and two bags. "Want me to help?"

She breathed heavily, her arms shaking. "Please."

He was at her side in an instant, scooping the girl up into his arms. He held the room keys between his fingers, gesturing for Reagan to take them. "Separate rooms?" she asked, holding them up.

"I didn't want to overstep."

She nodded, without saying anything else and pointed to the elevator. They rode up to the third floor in silence, Gunner staring down at the little girl in his arms.

"I always forget how big she's gotten," Reagan said as the door opened and they walked out into the hall. "She still seems so little to me until I go to carry her."

Gunner tried to smile, though he felt a lump grow in his throat at realizing he'd never get to hold the baby his daughter had once been. This was the smallest version of her he'd ever know. They walked into the hotel room and Reagan pulled back the sheet so Gunner could place Nora into bed. He pulled her tennis shoes off and covered her up, kissing her forehead awkwardly.

"Oh, crap, I forgot the other bags from the trunk. Can you wait with her? I'll go get them," Reagan told him.

"No way, you're not going out there alone. I'll go get the bags. You stay with Nora."

He grabbed a room key from the side table and disappeared through the door before she could protest. After pressing the button and waiting for the golden doors to open, he walked onto the elevator. On his way to the car, he fiddled with the room key, sliding it between his fingers. He grabbed the three bags from the car's trunk, slinging them over his shoulders.

Before he went in, he stopped, opening the car door and then the glove box, and grabbed his pack of cigarettes. He lit one quickly, touching it to his lips and inhaling. The warm, familiar tingle filled his lungs. It was the first cigarette he'd had in several weeks. The stress of his situation had him craving the nicotine he'd once loved so much. Or maybe it was something else he was craving. He threw the butt down on the black pavement and smashed it with the toe of his boot.

When he made it back to the hotel room, he knocked carefully. She opened the door, taking a bag from him. "Thanks," she said. In his absence, she had changed into flannel pajama pants and a t-shirt. Her hair looked freshly brushed.

"No problem," he answered when she looked back at him. "I guess this is my room." He pointed to the door beside the desk. "I'll leave you guys for the night. You should get some sleep, it's going to be an early morning."

"Gunner?" she called as he began to walk away.

"Yeah?" He turned back.

"Um, I just wondered...would you stay with me for a while? Until I fall asleep, maybe? We can watch TV or whatever. I'm just not used to being somewhere new. It makes me sort of nervous." She looked embarrassed to admit it.

He thought for a moment, his brain begging for sleep. "Okay, sure."

"Thank you." She closed her eyes, heaving a sigh of relief. "I know you're exhausted."

He tried to hide his yawn. "I'm all right."

She sat down on the bed but jumped back up immediately. "Oh, wait! I have a surprise for you."

"A surprise?" He yawned again, watching her run to her bag and dig through it. She produced a small red and white box, something he hadn't seen in years. "Cracker Jacks? You hate them." He eyed her suspiciously.

"I know. But Nora has her father's taste, apparently. They're her favorite too, so we keep them in the house." She handed him the box.

"I don't want to eat hers."

"Trust me," she said, pulling out three more boxes. "We have plenty."

Gunner smiled, tearing off the top and pouring a few into his mouth. She made her way to the bed again, sitting down carefully so as not to wake Nora. He walked to the chair across the room and sat.

"So, are you nervous to go back to New York?" she asked.

"Nervous? Why?"

"I mean...don't you ever get scared? Especially now that you know someone who died there. Lots of people die there.

I'm just...I guess I'm scared of new places, big cities, anything I don't know."

He shook his head. "New York doesn't scare me."

"Why? Because you're too big and bad for that?" she teased.

"No." He swallowed, too tired for a filter. "Because my biggest fear was losing you. And I already did that."

She looked down, obviously not expecting that answer. When she looked back up, her eyes were soft. "I've never wanted to go back in time so badly in my life."

"Tell me about it," he said casually, popping another Cracker Jack into his mouth.

"Didn't you ever think about calling? Or coming home? Even once?"

"Of course I did. I can't count the number of times I drove halfway home just to turn around. Or the times I dialed your number but chickened out and hung up. I couldn't do it. Especially after they died. I couldn't face you, couldn't face the town, my mother—it was all too much."

"I came to their memorial service, you know. For Holly, of course. But also because I wanted to see you...I thought you'd be there. When you weren't, that's when I knew you weren't ever coming home."

His eyes went dark. "I hated him, Rae. I still do some days. I hated him for taking you from me. I hated him for always being better than I was." He shook his head. "How sick is it to hold a grudge against a dead guy?"

She stared at him, unblinking. "In my head, Gavin is still the reason for my broken heart. He's the reason Nora has grown up without a father. So, if you're sick, I'm sick too."

He offered a small smile. "Maybe we *are* meant for each

other." When she didn't respond, he went on. "Hey, I have to ask, what would you have done if I told you I did have something to do with the fire?"

She sucked in a sharp breath, touching her stomach. "Why?"

"I've always told you I'm not a good guy. I wasn't lying when I said I didn't kill my family. That doesn't mean I couldn't have prevented it."

"What does that mean?"

"It doesn't matter, I guess. It's just...it'll always feel like I could've done something to stop it from happening. Gia begged me to take her with me, but she wanted Gavin to go too. I was so mad at him, I couldn't look past it and see how much they needed me."

"Gunner, your dad blew up your house in a drunken rage. I only asked if you had anything to do with it because of the timing. I knew how mad you were, but I always knew you weren't capable of anything that horrible. No matter what you did or didn't do, it wasn't your fault. You couldn't have saved them."

"I would've come to their funerals if I'd known," he said quietly. "I threw out my phone when I was leaving town and when I got to New York I didn't give anyone my new phone number. I didn't find out until they'd been dead for a few weeks." He'd never admitted that to anyone.

"That's...awful," she whispered, staring at him in horror.

"My dad may have been a horrible drunk and Gavin may have ruined my life, but they were still my family. I may never forgive them for what they did, but I would've come to say goodbye. Especially to Gia. Most of the time, she was my only friend. Until you came along."

"Would you come over here?" she asked, patting the spot beside her.

He did as she asked without thought. "Tell me more about Nora." The ride from Dale to Louisville had been filled with stories of their daughter, things he'd missed. But eight hours couldn't make up for seven years worth of memories.

"Hmmm," she thought out loud, "well, she's smart. Top of her class, according to her teachers."

"Having a teacher for a mother will do that to you."

"Yeah, well, she loves to read like her dad."

He loved the way that word sounded rolling off her tongue. "She does?"

"Oh, yes. She's a huge reader. And she didn't get that from me. I hadn't read a book in years until I had her. We're reading Lemony Snicket together right now."

"What else?"

"She's opinionated and bold and unafraid...of everything." She laughed. "That's not always a good thing. She's just...amazing, Gunner. Honestly, she's the best thing that ever happened to me."

He played with a loose thread on the comforter. "I'm so glad. I never thought I'd be a dad. I never thought I wanted to. I didn't exactly have a role model father to show me the ropes, so even if I became a dad, I didn't think I'd be worth anything as one. And, after I found out, well...it took me a while to warm up to the idea, but I'm so happy to get to know her."

"You're good with her." She pressed her lips together, her eyes squinting as if she were smiling.

"I'm glad you think so."

"You've always been good, Gunner. You took care of me like no one ever had. You're a nurturer. You're going to be a natural father."

"You remember a better version of me than I do."

She touched a piece of his hair, rubbing his cheek. It was the first time she'd touched him in what felt like so long. "You aren't the monster you think you are. I wish you could see yourself the way I do."

"How's that?"

She closed her eyes, her hand still on his face and for a second he thought she was going to kiss him. "The first time I talked to you...you helped me get home on one of the most humiliating days of my life. You didn't make me feel embarrassed. You weren't a typical guy about something you really could have been. You didn't owe me anything, Gunner. You just...you just did it because you could. You hardly knew me, and yet, you helped me."

He blinked slowly, lost in her words, remembering the start of their love. "The next time," she went on, "you saved me from being attacked by a horrible boy at a party, even though it ruined your evening. You made me feel safe and you helped me get home without making a fool of myself. You took me to prom and made it one of the most beautiful nights I'll probably ever experience. You danced with me even though it wasn't the cool thing to do. You went to my graduation and you clapped when they called my name even though you were supposed to wait. You were the first boy I ever let into my heart and you didn't take advantage of that. You were the best part of the years we spent together. You were kind to me, respectful of everything I wanted and everything I didn't. For a while there, I think you stopped seeing yourself as the troublemaking bad boy and became the man you were meant to be. You just need to see him again," she said. "*You are good, Gunner.*" She stressed her words, her face close to his.

"I'm good when I'm around you because you deserve it. There's a difference in pretending to be good for you and actually being good."

"The fact that you even care what I deserve says otherwise." She pursed her lips, their eyes locked together.

"I'll always care what you deserve, Rae." She stared at him, her hand caressing his face, eyes dancing between his. "So, I hope Jesse is that." He broke the tension, looking away.

She blinked, suddenly aware of what was happening, and moved her hand. "Gunner, Jesse is a good guy. But that doesn't mean I love him like I love you."

"Love? Not loved?" His heart leapt at her words.

"It'll always be love with us. For me, anyway." She sighed.

"For me too," he whispered instantly, waiting for her to finish her thought.

"It's like...no matter how much bad there was between us, how much I hated you when you left...I can't forget how much I need you in my life. Even if it is too late."

He stroked her hand where it rested on her knee. "It's only too late if you let it be."

"Jesse doesn't deserve this," she told him, though she didn't pull away.

"What about what you deserve?"

"You're the one with all of these wild notions about what I deserve."

"You deserve happiness. Whether or not that's with me."

"Jesse came along at a time when I was really alone. Nora was getting ready to start school and I was struggling with doing it all by myself. He stepped into the spot where you should have been and I'll always be thankful for that. He's good to me. He takes care of us. I'm comfortable with him. I don't have to worry like I did before. But comfortability doesn't always equal happiness."

"What does?"

She laced her fingers through his. "This. Sitting here with you after all these years. Having our little family together. Seeing you with our daughter. Being able to sit in a strange hotel, in a town I've never been to, and feel completely at home because you're here. That's happiness, Gunner. And I'm so scared to say goodbye to that. I'm so scared I'm going to wake up to you gone again."

He leaned into her without reservation, resting his forehead on hers. She closed her eyes, sucking in a sharp breath. "I'm not going anywhere ever again," he promised her, his heart racing.

She leaned her chin forward, their lips brushing cautiously. He kissed her gently at first, amazed at how quickly she fell into his arms. He had been waiting for this, he realized, since he laid eyes on her that first night back in town. A weight escaped his chest in the form of a breath, everything suddenly feeling right.

He ran his hands through her hair slowly, their breaths syncing as their kiss grew. "Gunner," she whispered his name once, and then again more sharply, pulling away.

"What is it?"

"I owe Jesse more than this."

His heart sank.

"I want to be with you. But I'm engaged to another man. A good man. I owe him a breakup that isn't done after I make out with my ex-boyfriend."

He nodded. "You're right." God, he didn't want her to be right.

"I'm sorry. I really, really am."

"I know."

"As soon as we get back to Dale, I'll tell Jesse everything. But, until then, we have to be respectful of our relationship."

Again, he nodded. "I love you."

She smiled. "It feels good to hear you say that again."

Remembering the last time he said it, his face grew warm. "And you love me too?" he coaxed.

She laughed. "Oh, how the roles have reversed." She touched his lips. "I love you back. Always have, always, always will."

He kissed her fingertips. "Always."

TWENTY-SIX

GUNNER

When they arrived in the city, Gunner pulled his car into a parking garage. Nora was fascinated by the city, its tall buildings, many people, and bustling streets. Reagan, meanwhile, looked terrified.

He touched her leg. "It's okay," he assured her. They climbed out of the car and Gunner led them through the back entrance of his building, their bags in hand. They walked up the flight of stairs and onto his floor. Gunner stopped in front of the green door, squinting his eyes as they adjusted to the fluorescent lights. There was a white folded piece of paper taped to the front of his door.

"What's that?" Reagan asked.

Gunner pulled it from the door, his heart dropping.

You're in danger.

HE CONSIDERED TRYING to hide it from her, but he knew there was no use. He handed it over, opening the door and ushering them into the apartment. It was just as he left it, though the air was a bit stale from being unoccupied for the time he'd been gone. He was slightly embarrassed for them to see the messy bachelor pad he called home.

"What do you think this means?" Reagan asked, her voice shaky with concern.

"It's fine," he said, sitting the bags down on the coffee table, though he felt anything but fine. He picked up a few empty water bottles and tossed them into the trash. "This isn't a bad neighborhood." He smiled at Nora. "What do you want to do first?"

"Can we watch TV?" she asked excitedly.

"*TV*?" He scoffed. "No, we're in New York City. This may be the only time you're ever here. We have to go to Central Park, get a slice of giant pizza, see Times Square, meet a celebrity. Don't you know how much fun New York is?"

The girl shook her head.

"Well, I'm not letting you leave until you love it as much as I do." He rubbed her head playfully, pointing to the remote. "We'll do TV tonight since it's late but tomorrow we're going to explore the city." She rubbed her eyes, yawning, and grabbed the remote from the arm of the couch. "Make yourself at home."

"Where's your restroom?" Reagan asked and Gunner

directed her to it. He walked to the kitchen, opening the fridge. It was no use. He knew there would be no food there. He hardly kept anything in the house—choosing to eat out for almost every meal. He was right, of course. He stared apprehensively at the two cans of soda, one jar of hot sauce, and what looked like an old orange.

When she reappeared, she'd brushed her hair and her face was red as if she'd just washed it.

"This place is..."

"Nice?" he offered.

"Small," she said with laughter in her voice.

"Yeah, New York's real estate is a bit different than Dale's."

"You probably pay more a month here than we pay in a year."

"It's not too bad," he assured her, though he knew she was right. "Anyway, I'm going to run down and grab us something for dinner. What does Nora like?"

"What?" Her eyes filled with fear. "No, you can't leave us here alone."

"I don't have anything here for us to eat. We've been living on fast food and cracker jacks for two days. We need something real. They have a great little italian place right across the street. You can watch me leave the building. You'll have your eye on me the whole time. Just keep the doors locked. There's no reason to get her out so late. She's safer here." Reagan looked uneasy, biting her lip. "I promise you it'll be fine. I'll be gone ten minutes."

She nodded finally, though she didn't respond.

"Just stay here," he said. "Lock and deadbolt the door behind me and don't answer the door for anyone but me. Go to the window, I'll be right down there on the street. You can see the restaurant from here."

"Hurry," she begged, looking back to Nora who was happily watching the television, oblivious to anything else going on.

"What does she like? Spaghetti? Alfredo?"

"Pizza?" Reagan asked.

"You let her eat pizza? I thought you wanted organic everything?"

She rolled her eyes. "Oh, I like healthy food just as much as the next person, but I'm still a mom. Kids love pizza."

"I can do pizza," he said, kissing the top of her head. He walked out the door, listening for the lock to click before he walked down the stairs. He made his way out of the building and turned to look up at his window. She was there, watching him. He held a hand up, waving quickly, and then pointed to the restaurant where he was headed.

Just as he reached the pizza place, he stopped, pulling his phone out of his pocket and calling Nigel.

"Hey, it's Gunner James."

"Gunner! Where've you been? You dropped off the radar there for a bit. I've already got three jobs lined up for tonight. What side of town are you on?"

"No," Gunner answered, "that's actually why I'm calling. I'm not going to be taking on any more jobs. I'm calling to put in my notice."

"What?" He sounded as though he were eating something, but that didn't hide his shock. "Why?"

"I'm leaving the city. I won't be here much longer, I just came back to get a few things. Tie up some loose ends."

"I'm sorry to see you go, my friend. Will I get a chance to see you before you leave?"

"I hope so. I'm still trying to get everything worked out. Hey, listen...the night I left town, the third, there was a murder in my building. Can you check and see if any of our guys cleaned it?"

"Uh, sure." He strained a bit as if he were standing up and then Gunner heard him flipping through papers. "Yep, looks like Ryan did. Why?"

"Does he have anything mentioned on the report? Anything suspicious? Strange?" He was working solely on a hunch.

"Hm, nope, sorry, Gunner. It does say the boyfriend signed off on the cleaning, so maybe check with him? What exactly are you looking for?"

"Boyfriend? She had a boyfriend?"

"According to this. Boyfriend was the one who hired us."

"Does it give a name?"

"Fletcher Denali?" he read aloud. "Ring any bells?"

"Not particularly," he said under his breath. "Never mind. Okay, thanks, Nigel. I'll talk to you soon, bud."

"Okay, take care, Gunner. If you're ever back in the city, give me a call. There's always a dead guy ready for ya." He laughed at his own joke.

Gunner hung up, walking into the restaurant and ordering a large pizza. He hadn't thought to check on toppings so he went with half pepperoni and half cheese to be safe.

When he walked back into his building a few minutes later, he stopped by Hermy's apartment, knocking loudly.

The elderly man appeared at once. "Gunner, welcome back. Is everything all right?"

"I just had a question. Was there anyone else on Holly's lease?"

"The dead girl?" he asked.

"Yes," Gunner answered, though he hated calling her that.

"No, just her. Why?"

"You're sure?"

"Positive. I had to answer that question for the police."

"She didn't have a boyfriend living with her?"

"Well, there was a young man who packed up all of her things when I signed over her lease to the new tenants. I don't know what his relationship was with the girl."

"You've already filled her apartment?"

"It's New York, Gunner," he smiled innocently. "It's not exactly hard to find new tenants."

"Well, good," he said, "because I'll be turning in my notice to you soon. I'm having to move back home."

"I'm sorry to hear that," he said kindly. "You were one of my few decent tenants, but don't repeat that. Anyway, is there anything else I can do for you? I was about to turn in for the night."

"Just one more thing. Did you get the name of the man who packed up her stuff?"

"Well, no. Should I have?"

Gunner sighed. "No, thanks, Hermy. Sorry to have bothered you. Have a good night." He turned and jogged up the staircase without another word. When he reached the apartment, he was surprised to see another note. He grabbed it from the door quickly and read:

Welcome Home

THAT WAS IT. Two simple words that instantly sent chills up his spine. He wadded up the note, stuffing it in his pocket and deciding not to worry Reagan with it any more. He knocked on the door. "It's me," he said softly. He heard her footsteps and then each of the three locks turning before the door crept open.

She looked relieved to see it truly was him. "Pizza," he announced, holding up the box. "See, look, we're already starting on our New York to-do list."

Nora squealed, grabbing a piece of pepperoni as soon as he sat the box down. He couldn't help but smile—she certainly had gotten his tastes.

"Hey," he said to Reagan as he walked into the kitchen, headed toward the bedroom. She followed him. He slipped his shirt over his head and grabbed a clean one from the drawer. Her eyes flickered over his chest and he smirked. "Did Holly have a boyfriend?"

"Not that I know of." Her gaze went back to his. "Why?"

"Does the name Fletcher Denali sound familiar to you?"

"No. *Why?*" She repeated the 'why' with frustrated worry.

"That's the guy who paid for Holly's apartment to be cleaned. It's usually a husband, boyfriend, brother, friend, roommate, something. I thought if we could find him, maybe he could give you some more insight into her final days."

"How do you know his name?"

"I called in a favor with my boss."

"I wish I knew who it was. Maybe her dealer?" she said somberly.

"Maybe. I've never seen a dealer stick around and pay for our services, though."

She frowned. "My sister was my best friend, but I swear it's like I didn't know her at all."

"Mom! Gunner!" Nora yelled from the living room. "Come on!"

He grabbed a pair of ball shorts, waiting for her to leave. "I'm just going to change real quick. Go on out and get something to eat."

"Nothing I haven't seen before," she said casually, but turned and sauntered from the room anyway. He ripped his jeans off, pulling on his shorts, and throwing away the note in the small wastebasket beside his dresser.

He hurried into the living room, snatching a piece of pizza and sinking down onto the couch between them. "Hey," he said, pointing to the slice in Nora's hand. "That's the piece I wanted."

She smiled, pizza sauce sticking to the corners of her mouth. "Boy, is it good." She took a large bite in spite of him, giggling loudly.

He laid his pizza down, reaching over as if he were going to grab hers but instead landed on her stomach, tickling her. She laughed loudly, holding her pizza over his head. "*Okay, okay, okay. Stop! Stop!*" She laughed more. Her laughter made him want to continue. Beside them, Reagan was grinning, snacking on her own piece. "*Stop, please!*" Nora begged through her tears of laughter. "*Dad, stop!*"

The room fell silent and he stopped tickling as the word

left her mouth. She sat up straight, her face sobering. "I'm sorry."

He looked at her, she did indeed look apologetic. "Don't be sorry," he said.

"Is it all right to call you that?"

"You can call me anything you want, Nor," he said seriously. "But only when you're ready."

He wasn't sure he was ready. Not really. But it felt good to have a title, to be something to someone. He could only hope to be worthy of that name. Worthy of the little girl who would call him that.

Nora didn't respond, turning up the TV and settling in. After a few moments, Reagan rested her head on his shoulder, beginning to yawn, and pretty soon Nora followed suit. The two girls slowly drifted off to sleep, obviously feeling safe in his arms and Gunner couldn't help but think of the other title he hoped to carry one day. The one that traditionally came before 'Dad'. But then, he was getting ahead of himself.

TWENTY-SEVEN

GUNNER

The next morning, Gunner awoke to the sun shining in through his blinds. Used to the blackout curtains in his bedroom, he felt blinded. He leaned forward on the couch, sliding the girls' heads off of his shoulders and placing them back down carefully. Reagan stirred just for a second, but they were both back asleep in moments.

He walked to the kitchen, grabbing the coffee pot. Before he could flick on the water, he froze, listening carefully. He heard the quiet, cautious footsteps approaching his door. Setting the coffee pot on the counter, he walked toward the door and stared out the clouded peephole.

A woman stood in the hallway facing his apartment, her dark hair hanging in her eyes. He couldn't see her well. He pressed his hands to the metal of the locks, turning them slowly. Warning her that he was onto her would be detrimental to his plan. The third lock, the deadbolt, made a loud 'click' as it slid open and he prayed she hadn't heard it. In an instant, the girl turned, running away from the door. He swung it open, stepping out into the hallway. "Wait!" he yelled after her. A white paper was taped to his door again, but he didn't have time to grab it. "Wait!" he yelled again, grabbing hold of her arm as she reached the top of the staircase, ready to descend. She fought his grasp, pinching and prodding his fingers off of her bicep. Finally, she gave up and turned around to face him in defeat.

He dropped her arm, taking a step back. It was as if the breath had been ripped from his lungs by ice cold fingers. "What..." he said, shaking his head. Nothing made sense. It wasn't possible. Her once raven black hair had been badly lightened to reveal a rusty brown color. Her face had aged, now filled with wrinkles, dark spots, and more breakouts than before. Her hair was dull, her skin lifeless. Everything about her had changed. And yet, he knew her the moment their eyes met. She was the same. So different and still so familiar.

He stared at her, unable to find the words to say everything on his mind.

Finally, realizing he wouldn't be the first to speak, she smirked, her eyes narrowing at him. "Hello, brother."

TWENTY-EIGHT

GUNNER

The ghost sat on his couch, staring back and forth between him, Reagan, and Nora.

"I just don't understand," he repeated for what must've been the hundredth time.

"You're supposed to be dead," Reagan agreed.

"I am dead," she said softly. "Well, Gia is anyway. I go by Fiona now."

"But why? Why and how?" He felt overwhelmed by the revelation. Everything he believed he had known had been ripped away from him.

"It's a long story," she said calmly. "One I'll explain to you both. But you have to swear you won't tell anyone you've seen me. Not ever."

"You were the one leaving me notes?" he asked, leaning forward in his seat.

"I wanted to warn you."

"About what?"

"You're in danger, Gunner. You all are."

Reagan touched Nora's shoulder. "Sweetheart, why don't you go take your shower?"

"I don't wanna," the girl argued.

"Please don't fuss, Nora."

The girl sighed, disappearing into the bathroom slowly.

"Why are we in danger?" Gunner asked once he could hear the water running.

"We've been watching you for a while. I just wanted to keep a check on you, see what was happening with your life. I don't think his intentions were so pure."

"What do you mean? Who's he?"

"Gavin. Or...well, Fletcher."

"Fletcher? As in Fletcher Denali? The boyfriend? Wait a second, are you saying Gavin's alive, too?"

"Yes," she said, "there's so much you don't know, Gun. So much. And you need to hear it all, but we don't have time, so I'm just going to have to throw the highlights at you. If he finds out I'm with you...that I've told you anything...we'll all be in even more danger."

"What the hell are you talking about, Gia?" he asked, his voice irritated.

"Gavin's bad now, Gunner. Ever since the fire, it's like he just snapped. I don't know how to explain it. After what he did to Reagan, he wanted you to be mad. He wanted to make you furious...maybe he even wanted you to break up, but you did the one thing he never planned for you to do when you left. You left us in that house, with that monster. And he's pissed, Gunner. He wants revenge. And I don't know how much longer I can protect you."

"What are you talking about? What he did to Reagan? You mean sleeping with her? He told you about that?"

She nodded.

"What do you mean he wanted me to be mad? Gavin was drunk. Reagan said he hadn't realized when he was doing that night."

"No, Gunner. He knew exactly what he was doing. When he came home that day, he told me all about it with perfect clarity. It was a deliberate act. I mean, sure, he was drunk so his judgement may have been impaired, but he was consciously acting on his decision."

"What decision?" Beside him, Reagan looked as though she were going to be sick. She wrapped her hands around her waist, rocking back and forth as she processed the new information. He pulled her into him, feeling anger bubbling in his stomach. He could've killed him if given the chance.

"He wanted to compete with you, Gunner. He wanted to win."

"So he...he raped me?" Reagan demanded, her voice hysterical.

Ignoring her question, Gia went on. "When he came home and found out you were gone...he was furious. Like, worse than I'd ever seen him. He planned out the fire before the day ended."

Gunner's body began shaking, his skin growing cold. "Gavin set the fire?"

"Yes." She nodded.

"Why would he want to kill you?"

"He didn't. He wanted to save us. Because he said you weren't going to."

"But the police found traces of your bodies, Momma said. They buried you."

"No, they found my watch and Gavin's belt, our shoes, some shreds of clothing. Whatever survived the fire. He started the fire in our room so they would be okay with not finding our bodies. They just had to find enough to be okay with labeling us as dead. It was kind of brilliant, actually."

"Brilliant? It's sick!" He felt dizzy.

"It was what had to be done."

"And what about Momma? Does she know about your plan? Does she know you're still alive?"

"No," she snapped.

"Why? She deserves to know the truth. She believes she buried everyone that day. She should know that wasn't the case."

"Momma can't know. No one can. Gavin would go to jail. For the fire, for faking our deaths, for murdering our father. He's our brother, Gun. I can't let that happen."

"Mom would keep your secret. She would protect you."

"No," she reiterated. "We can't trust anyone. I shouldn't have even come to you except that I'm really worried about what he's planning. He disappeared a few days after Holly died. I haven't seen him since. It's not like him to be gone for long and he took our car when he left so I have no way to find him."

"Holly?" Reagan asked, suddenly back focusing on the conversation. "My sister? Were you guys with Holly? She knew about you?"

"Yes," Gia answered her. "Holly and Gavin couldn't be kept apart. He felt so guilty about breaking her heart the way he did. He contacted her a few weeks after our funeral."

"Weeks? She's known that you are both alive for years? She never told me anything."

"She couldn't. We made her swear not to tell a soul."

"I thought we told each other everything," she said, her voice breaking. Gunner squeezed her shoulder.

"She didn't have a choice, Reagan." Gia's voice was harsher than Gunner would have liked.

"So, did Gavin know Holly was on drugs? Did you?"

"She wasn't on drugs. None of us are. Gavin used heroin as a way to cover up her death. When he found out she was pregnant, he panicked. She wanted to tell her family. She swore she would keep our secret, but Gavin knew that wasn't possible. He knew the baby would destroy everything we'd worked so hard for. Our freedom. She wouldn't have an abortion and Gavin couldn't figure out a solution. He loved her so much. But he was scared...he didn't want to go to jail. I don't think he really meant for it to happen. He hates himself for it."

"He didn't mean to...kill her?" Gunner asked, her words sounding so foreign to him. Then again, she was talking about the man who had burned down his home at only seventeen.

"No, he didn't. We just couldn't have people finding out about us. We couldn't have Momma finding out."

"Why Momma? You really think she'd tell your secret?"

"She hates us, Gunner. She'd kill us if she ever saw us again."

He shook his head, feeling Reagan continuing to quiver in fear beside of him. "She wouldn't. You saved her life."

"Don't you get it, Gunner? We didn't save her. We saved ourselves *from* her."

"What does that even mean? Once Dad was gone you were safe. You were all safe."

"*No,*" she stressed the word. "Dad was never the one we were afraid of, Gun. It was always Momma who hurt us."

"What?" he asked, unable to believe her. "No, it was Dad. You always said it was Dad."

"No. We didn't. Think back. You saw the bruises and assumed it was Dad. We just never corrected you because we didn't want things to get worse. We wouldn't tell the police with you because you had it all wrong. Momma was the monster, Daddy was just a drunk."

"That's not possible," he said, his chest growing increasingly tight with each breath.

"Gunner, don't you remember how mean she was? Don't you remember how she'd pull my hair when I annoyed her or pinch Gavin when he smarted off? And that was just in front of you. When you weren't around...it was the stuff from nightmares. She always told us she was doing it to protect us from Daddy. She said if he got his hands on us, it would've been much worse. But, truth be told, I don't know how. We believed her because she was our mother. We thought she loved us. But we left because we had no choice. And now, if she finds out what we did, I'm sure she'll kill us."

"Why would she want to hurt you?" he asked, feeling unsure. "Dad was mad because you weren't biologically his. What reason did Mom have?"

"I have no idea. Maybe it gave her something to do when she was bored; maybe she felt like we ruined her life. You were the golden boy. Her perfect son. We were proof that she'd made a mistake. We ruined her marriage, her life. She just hated us."

"Bullshit, Gia. I was never the golden boy, that was Gavin."

"Everywhere else, yes. He is handsome and athletic and popular, but at home, you were the one mom loved the best. You had to see that," she said, urging him to agree.

He rubbed his forehead, thinking. "So, Dad never hurt you? Not a single time?"

"Never."

"I just...don't understand. Mom had bruises herself half the time."

"She did those to herself. She'd bang her face into the counter, hit her own head with the coffee pot. She wanted it to be believable. She was crazy, Gunner. When Daddy would sober up, she'd convince him he'd been the one to do it. He never knew the truth. We were too scared to ever argue."

"What the hell?" It was literally as if she'd been reading from a book. The story was rolling off her tongue, as unbelievable and wild as if it were a movie, and yet he could see the fear in her eyes. "How could I have missed that?"

"It doesn't matter. You aren't to blame. But we don't have time to dwell on that. Right now, we have to find Gavin and keep him out of trouble. We have to keep him away from you. Away from Dale in general. He knows, or at least suspects, that you went home for Holly's funeral. I'm sure that's where he's headed. To find you. He's off the rails. I don't know what he's planning."

"It's been eight years since *he* ruined *my* life. What on earth could he possibly want to hurt me for?" Gunner asked angrily.

"He blames you for it, Gunner. All of it. The fire. The

abuse. Us having to run. Holly's death. If you hadn't left that night, it could have been different."

"If he hadn't *raped* the love of my life—"

Reagan cut him off as the door to the bathroom opened and Nora reappeared. "I'm done," she announced, walking to the couch with a handful of dirty clothes. Reagan stood, taking the clothes and slipping them into a laundry bag she'd brought.

Gunner turned to Gia. "I never saw Gavin in Dale. Where else do you think he could be?"

"I honestly don't know. Before Holly moved here, we lived in Queens. And before that, we lived in South Carolina. Before that, Nashville, Tennessee. We've moved around a lot. We always have to keep moving."

He reached across the coffee table and grabbed his sister's hands. "No more moving. I'm going to keep you safe like I couldn't before."

"Gunner, you don't have to take care of me. I'm a grown woman."

"You're my baby sister first," he told her. "I should've protected you years ago."

"Don't blame yourself," she said, shaking her head. "I should've been honest with you about what was happening. I was just scared. I didn't want it to get worse."

"I know," he said, rubbing her hand. Just then, his phone began ringing in his pocket. He pulled it out, staring at the screen, and growled. "Speak of the devil."

"Gavin?" Gia asked anxiously.

"No. It's Momma." He slid his finger across the screen. "Hello?"

"Gunner?" she asked, her voice sounding hoarse.

"Momma? What is it?" He couldn't help but feel protective over her despite his anger.

"I don't want to bother you."

"What's going on?" he asked again.

"I know you're busy. I just wanted you to know I'm going in for another round of chemo today. You asked me to keep you informed, so I am. They found more cancer. It's spreading worse than before." She said it casually, as if she were telling him about the weather. "I thought you'd want to know."

"What? Since when?"

"I just got the call. I did it alone last time...I don't know if you want to come home. I can handle it alone again. But I wanted to let you know what was going on. I'd like to see you again before I die."

"Don't be dramatic," he said, a lump in his throat. "You made it through before, you'll be fine this time, right?"

"I don't think so, Gun. It's made it to the bone now, which was what they were afraid of. They don't seem to think..." She took a sharp breath. "I won't be here for much longer."

"I'll be home soon."

TWENTY-NINE

GUNNER

When they pulled into his mother's lot the next day, the car was filled with tension. Gia was visibly shaking in the backseat, despite Gunner's promise that he wouldn't let anything happen to her. An unfamiliar red car sat in a parking spot.

"That's Gavin," Gia gasped, seeing it at the exact time Gunner had. "I was right. He's here."

"Stay here." He turned around in his seat, facing the many eyes that were locked on him. "Lock the doors when I leave and do not get out of the car. Not for any reason. I'm going to go in and make sure he isn't hurting Momma. I need to find out what he wants."

"It could be a trap, Gunner," Reagan said, her eyes wide with fear. "Let's just go get the police."

"No," he said firmly. "Not yet. I don't want Gia to get into trouble."

"He's dangerous, Gunner," Gia said. "I don't know. Maybe we should wait."

"I'll be okay," he said firmly. "Just promise me you'll stay here. If anything happens, if I'm in there too long, you need to leave. Protect each other."

"Gunner—"

"Promise me," he demanded, his eyes on Reagan.

"I promise," Gia said finally.

Gunner leaned across, kissing Reagan on the lips. "I love you," he said. "I know we aren't doing that yet, but I do."

"I love you back," she told him.

Nora leaned up in the seat, gasping. "Did you just kiss my mom?" she demanded, her nose scrunched up as if she'd smelled something gross.

"Yep, I sure did," Gunner said, kissing Nora's forehead. "And I'm kissing you too, kiddo. You guys be safe."

As he started to open the door, Gia reached up and grabbed his hand. "I never wanted any of this. I just wanted to be free of her," she said, her wild eyes burning into his.

"I know," he said.

"Remember Gunner, no one can know I'm alive," she warned.

"It's going to be okay. I'm just going to get Gavin. I won't tell Momma anything."

He climbed out of the car before anyone could protest. "Twenty minutes," he called over his shoulder before shutting the door and walking up onto the porch. He didn't look back. Couldn't.

He pulled open the screen door, not bothering to knock and went into the house. "Momma?" he called. She was sitting in her old recliner, an afghan wrapped around her small body. Her skin was pale white, cheeks more sunken in than before. Her face was coated in sweat as if she were running a fever.

"Gunner?" she asked, her face lighting up when she saw him.

He rushed to her side, touching her hands. They were ice cold. "Where is he?"

"Where's who?" she asked.

Before he could answer, he heard the voice he hadn't heard in years, the voice he never thought he'd hear again.

"Hello, brother," Gavin's hatred-filled voice rang out from behind him. Gunner spun around.

"What are you doing here?" he demanded, his muscles tensing. His once blond hair was now a jet black, nearly the color of Gunner's. His arms were thinner, he'd lost most of the muscle he'd boasted in high school.

"I'm paying a visit to our dear old mom," he said, a menacing smile growing on his face.

"What did you do to her?" he asked angrily.

"I'm fine, Gunner," she answered, her voice breathy. "Honestly, it's just the chemo. Your brother couldn't hurt me."

"Shut up," Gavin snapped, rubbing his face. He looked exhausted, agitated.

"When's the last time you slept, Gav?" Gunner asked, taking a step toward him.

Ignoring him, Gavin's gaze remained locked on their mother. "I would gladly hurt you. But I need answers." He stepped forward.

Gunner stepped in between them, his hands up. He noticed the fists Gavin was making. "Woah, wait. Answers about what? You don't want to hurt her. You don't. I know you're mad, but it will only make things worse for you."

"You know...you know I'm mad?" He laughed hysterically. Manically even. "You couldn't possibly know anything, Gun. You couldn't because you never cared. You never bothered to stay around."

"Gavin, I know you're mad that I left. I know you're mad about Holly."

"Don't you say her fucking name, man!" he screamed, his temper flaring up even more. His body shook, the veins in his forehead poking out.

"I'm sorry," Gunner said, his hands up. "Let's just go, okay? Let's just leave Mom out of this. Gia is out in the car. We're going to talk this all out."

"Gia?" His eyes grew wide. "What are you talking about?"

"Gia's here. She's worried about you."

"Gia wouldn't have come for me."

"That's ridiculous. Of course she would."

"No!" he screamed. "No. *I'll kill her if I see her, she knows that.*" He darted for the door.

Gunner jumped in front of him. "What are you talking about?" He grabbed his brother's shoulders, their strength now closer to an even match. "You aren't killing anyone."

"Move out of my way." He shoved him out of the way, but Gunner was back in an instant.

"No. I'm not going to let you hurt her. What's going on? What answers are you looking for?" he begged, struggling to keep Gavin from the door.

"I need to find Gia. I thought Mom knew where she was," he said, throwing arms and fists Gunner's way. "I thought she'd come running home after she left. She had no one else to turn to. She could never be alone. You were gone. It had to be Momma." Gunner continued struggling to hold him back, trying to understand what he was saying. Suddenly, his fist slammed into Gunner's cheek and Gunner groaned, tasting blood.

"Stop it, right now!" their mother screamed from her chair. "Both of you. Can't you see how your fighting is upsetting your mother?"

"Shut up!" Gavin yelled at her. "No one cares if you're upset, you stupid old bitch. You're just as responsible for Holly's death as Gia. I hate you!" He was reaching hysterics now. He stopped struggling against Gunner, and charged at their mother.

"You stupid boy." Their mother cackled as he ran toward her, seemingly unafraid. "I'm glad she's dead," she said hatefully. "That's what you get, thinking you could run away from me."

Gunner turned, surprised by her evil words. "It's true?" he asked. "You really were the one all along? The one who hurt them?"

Gavin grabbed her shirt, pulling at it so it dug into her neck. He froze, awaiting her next move. She frowned as if nothing was happening, looking at him innocently. "Now, baby...I only did what I had to do."

"You had to abuse your children?" Gunner cried, not recognizing the woman in front of him. "You were their mother...our mother." He walked to them, pulling her shirt from his hands and helping Gavin to stand up straight. Tears had begun forming in his eyes as his mother's voice carried on coldly.

"I fed you. I kept a roof over your head. Just because I had to put them in their place every once in a while doesn't make me a bad mother."

"Put us in our place?" Gavin lunged at her again. "You sick—"

The woman screamed, falling from her chair dramatically before he'd even touched her. It was all an act. Gunner realized, then, it always had been. She'd just needed someone to pity her, and stupidly, he'd done just that. "Call the police, Gunner. Call them and tell him what he's doing to me. Call them."

Gunner pulled Gavin back, both of them staring down at her. "Gia told me everything, Momma. I'm sorry, I can't help you anymore."

"What are you gonna do, Gunner? Surely you can't hate your own mother?" she asked, her eyes wide, struggling to catch her breath. The excitement had caused her to begin coughing. She leaned over, hurling up the scanty contents of her stomach.

Gunner took a step back, unable to move. "You're no mother to us anymore," he said. "Maybe you never really were." It wasn't meant to be as harsh as the words sounded, but still they were true. The woman on the floor wasn't the woman he'd loved so much growing up. And somehow, that disconnect allowed him to look away from her when she needed him the most.

"We should go," he told Gavin. "I know you want Momma dead. And I know you want me dead, too. But Gia is waiting in the car. She just wants to know that you're safe. I owe her that much. We can figure the rest out later."

"Why would I want you dead?" he asked, his face confused.

"I know you tried to rape Reagan," he said, his jaw tight. "And that's something I'll never forgive you for. And I know you hate me for leaving. But I didn't know what she was doing. Or...maybe I did, in a way, and I didn't care. And that's something you're allowed to never forgive me for. But you can't do this. You can't kill any more. Not Momma, not me. Two deaths are enough."

"What are you talking about, Gunner? I never killed anyone. And I certainly never tried to rape Reagan. I was drunk that night, man. I would never do that to you."

"Come on, Gavin. I know about Dad. And I know about Holly."

From the ground, their mother spit on the carpet, wiping her mouth with her sleeve. She slowly climbed back into her seat, her eyes on them as if she were watching a movie. It took her a long time to sit down, her shaking growing more fierce. She was trying desperately to coerce a reaction from them.

"What are you talking about? Dad? Holly?" His voice was growing increasingly agitated.

"Gia told me what happened. About the baby. And the fire."

"What did she tell you?" he asked, looking at Gunner like he was speaking another language.

"That you...she told me that you killed them, Gav."

Gavin took a step back as if he'd been punched in the chest. "She...what? She said that I...I..." He blinked rapidly, fighting back tears, his mouth opened as he tried to speak. "No, Gunner, you've got it all wrong."

"What do you mean?"

"It wasn't me that killed them."

"Who was it?" Gunner asked, his insides growing cold as he feared he knew the answer.

"It was Gia. All of it was Gia."

"What?" He shook his head. "No."

"Gia started the fire. She was pissed that you left. She killed Dad. She wanted to kill Mom too, but we didn't know she hadn't made it to bed yet. And I could never…never have hurt Holly. I loved her. I loved her so much. We were gonna have a baby." He teared up, his chin quivering. "We were gonna have a family. Gia couldn't stomach it. She couldn't let there be a chance of anyone finding out that we were alive." His eyes darted to their mother. "Because of her. Because she was terrified of what she would do."

"You're saying Gia killed…everyone?"

"She's bad, Gunner. She's just lost herself. I thought she was starting to come around, but then the evil was back, just like the night of the fire. The moment she found out about the baby, she was the Gia who killed our father all over again. And then, she disappeared. I haven't seen her in days. I stayed in New York to clean up Holly's apartment, to say goodbye to her since I knew I couldn't come to the funeral, but now I have to find her. I have to catch her before she kills anyone else. Especially you. Now that you know we're alive, she's going to try to kill you, too. No one can know about us, Gunner."

His words went straight to Gunner's chest, sucking the air from his lungs. His knees grew weak, the hair on his arms standing up as he remembered her words. *No one can know I'm alive.*

"What is it?" Gavin asked, sensing his panic.

"Oh my god," Gunner bellowed, running for the door at full speed. He shoved the screen door open, hearing it bash into the wall behind him, but he wasn't focusing. He stared at the parking lot. At the exact spot where he'd left the car. At the empty tire tracks in the spot where it had just been.

No.

THIRTY

GIA
THE NIGHT OF HOLLY'S DEATH

Gavin, Gia, and Holly sat in the small apartment, staring into space.

"You have to have an abortion," Gia said finally.

"What?" Gavin demanded. "No way."

"You have to, Gav. Don't you see how dangerous this is?"

Holly covered her stomach defensively. "I'm not having an abortion. Not a chance. We can run away. We can leave the country. Or I can go back home and tell them I got knocked up by some random guy in college. My parents have money. I don't need someone to raise this baby with me."

"You aren't doing this alone," Gavin argued.

"Are you two hearing yourselves right now? This is a baby we're talking about. A living, breathing baby. We have been on the run for eight years, Gav. Eight years. Holly, you only see us part of the time. I mean, we appreciate you renting this

apartment for us and all, but you still have school and a life. And sure, you can say you don't need our help now, but what happens when you're suffering from sleep exhaustion and you're lonely and the baby has no father and Gavin can never ever come around? Are you going to bring the baby on the run with us? You can't even get married because we're legally dead. So, we resort to stealing or working under the table. What about that?"

"I know it's going to be complicated—" she began.

"You don't know the half of it. The bottom line is that if you have this baby, you're putting us all at risk. It's not worth it."

"You don't get to make this call, Gia. I'm sorry. We're having it. We'll figure everything else out as it comes, but we are having this baby. So, get on board or get out." Gavin's words were bullets, striking her hard and fast.

"Excuse me?"

"You heard me," he fired at her. "This place is in Holly's name, not yours. So, if you aren't going to help us figure this all out, you can just leave."

"You're going to risk our lives, our family, for her? For a baby you've never met?"

"She's my family now." He touched her stomach. "They are."

"I think I need to get some air," Gia said, standing up.

"Where are you going?" Gavin asked, his tone changing suddenly. "We don't want you to leave. We want you to be a part of this."

"You just made it abundantly clear that I am not a part of this, Gav. And so, that's that." She opened the heavy green door and slammed it shut with a bang. No one chased after

her. She walked past the door where she knew Gunner would be sleeping, if he were home. He worked strange hours. They'd started studying him to make sure not to cross paths. She considered knocking on his door, throwing her arms around the only brother who might still care about her. She was alone for the first time in her life and she hated the way that felt.

Being a twin was a strange thing—you spent so much of your life with this one other person. It was the strongest connection she could imagine. Stronger than marriage. Or family of any other kind. She couldn't allow herself to lose Gavin. She needed a plan.

She walked down the steps, banging on the door she'd seen junkies frequenting.

After a few moments, a skinny man with red hair and a patchy goatee opened the door. "Yeah?"

"I need something," she said simply, looking for pills or maybe pot to take the edge off. It had been years since she'd been high, always having to stay on alert, but if they weren't going to worry about getting caught, she figured she might as well enjoy her last few nights of freedom.

"Whatcha need, baby girl?" he asked, a smile creeping onto his face. His rotten teeth poked out from behind his lips.

She pulled out a wad of cash she'd stolen from Holly a few nights back. "Whatever this will buy."

He eyed her happily. "Step right in."

HEROIN. *H. Smack. Brown Sugar. There were many names for the drug she'd gotten from him, but she had no idea what on earth she was going to do with it. She'd done exactly as he'd told her to prepare it, but now she was at a loss. She wasn't actually going to shoot up, no matter how mad she was. She wasn't into hard drugs. In fact, she found them repulsive. But, as she stared at the needle in her hand, she began forming an idea.*

"That's enough to last you a few days," he'd told her, "so be careful. Build up a tolerance. That's not the stuff you want to start experimenting with, ya know?"

It was a warning, but also a prelude to the answer she'd been searching for.

Plan B. That's what she would call it. Her saving grace.

She walked back into the apartment as dawn had begun seeping in through the window. She walked into the bedroom, paying no attention to the blanket they'd left for her on the couch. That was her permanent resting place now. At one point, she and Gavin had rotated the bed. But, now that Holly was around more frequently, she was sequestered to the couch on a less-than-temporary basis.

She stared at them as they slept, their arms wrapped around each other. She could've been dying somewhere, or thrown into the back of a van, yet here they were, sleeping peacefully.

She pulled the comforter back, shoving the needle in between the girl's toes without hesitation. Once you'd killed someone, it really wasn't so hard to convince yourself to do it again. Holly jerked back, sitting up. "What did you do?" she screamed, half asleep, but it was too late.

"It didn't have to be like this," Gia informed her, holding the needle up into the air. Gavin sat up, looking at Holly's panicked face, and then, at Gia.

"What happened?" he demanded. Gia shrugged, waiting.

Watching. Gavin jumped from the bed, shaking her shoulders. "Gia, what did you do?"

On the bed, Holly had fallen limp, her body convulsing underneath the comforter. He hurried back to her side. "What was it? What did you give her?" He wrapped his arms around her, sobbing openly. "Call nine-one-one," he screamed. "Please don't do this." He hugged her, running his hands through her hair. "Please Gia, please call for help. Don't die on me, Hol, don't you dare die on me." He screamed and cursed, crying out for help that Gia had no intention of giving him. She watched as the girl died in his arms, Gavin helplessly crying out but unable to move from her side.

When it was over, he turned to her, his eyes filled with deep hatred. "I'm going to call the cops. I'm going to tell them everything you did."

"If you were going to call the cops, you already would have. You know as well as I do you'd be in jail along with me."

"You killed her in cold blood, Gia. Because...what? Because she was pregnant? Because I love her more than you?"

She slapped him across the face, dropping the needle onto the bed. "If you want to stay here and get arrested, Gavin, that's on you. One day, you'll see that I just saved us both. And maybe one day, you'll thank me. Until that day, don't contact me. We are through." She sauntered from the room, feeling practically giddy. Problem solved.

THIRTY-ONE

GUNNER
PRESENT DAY

"Where could she have gone?" he demanded, facing Gavin.

"I don't know," he said firmly. "I honestly don't."

Gunner grabbed his shirt, pulling him down an inch so they were nose to nose. "Tell me where she could be, damnit."

"Trust me, you don't want to find her."

"She has Reagan. And my daughter. We have to find her, Gavin. She's going to kill them."

Gavin went into action, pulling a set of keys from his pants. "Call nine-one-one," he shouted at him.

"What?" Gunner asked, climbing into the red car.

"I already lost Holly. We aren't going to lose anyone else. Call nine-one-one and have them track Reagan's phone."

Gunner dialed the number. "Nine-one-one, what's your emergency?"

"My girlfriend has been kidnapped."

"Okay, sir. I hear you. Do you know who has kidnapped your girlfriend? Do you believe she is in danger?"

"My sister kidnapped her. And yes, she's in danger. My sister killed her sister a few days ago."

If the woman was confused, she didn't let it show. "And when was the last time you saw your girlfriend?"

"Just a few minutes ago. My sister stole my car. It had my girlfriend and my seven-year-old daughter in it."

"There's a child in the car also?"

"Yes," Gunner confirmed as Gavin turned around a sharp curve. He grabbed the handle above his head to keep from sliding.

"Do you have any idea where they might be headed?"

"No."

"Okay, where are you now?"

"We're in Dale, Georgia. Headed east on Route 440 from the downtown square."

"Great. I'm dispatching police to that location. Are you able to pull over?"

"I'm not pulling over until we find them."

"I hear you, sir. This situation is better left for the police to handle. They are en route to your location now. Can you describe the car they are in?"

"It's a black Corsica, ninety-six model. Rusty. My sister has light brown hair, she'll be driving. Roughly one hundred and thirty pounds. Five foot three. My girlfriend has blonde hair, they're both in their late twenties. My girlfriend's name is Reagan Orrick. My sister is Gia James. Up until two days ago, I believed she was dead. She's a murderer. She's very dangerous. My daughter is Nora Orrick. She has black hair.

She's seven. I can give you my girlfriend's phone number if you can track her based on that." He shouted random facts into the phone, anything he could think of that might help.

"I'm taking all of these notes down and sharing them with our officers so they know what to look for. Can you tell us where they would've been leaving from?"

He gave her his mother's address. "I don't know where they could be going," he repeated, his voice cracking. "Please find them."

"I hear you, sir, we are going to do everything—"

He hung up the phone, interrupting her. "Where are we headed?" he asked Gavin, hoping his brother had a plan.

"To save your girl," he said, nodding his head to point straight up ahead. "She's taking them back."

"Back?"

"Back to where it all began. All of this."

He turned the corner and suddenly Gunner realized what Gavin was saying. "What? You think she's going to take them to the lakehouse?"

"Why not? It's empty now from what we've heard. Grandpa moved out of town after Grandma died, but they never sold the place. Gia still has the keys. We always talked about using it as a safehouse if we ever needed somewhere to hide. She's going to need somewhere secluded."

The thought made him sick to his stomach and he leaned forward in his seat. "Drive faster. I'm calling back to let them know where we're headed."

THEY PULLED up to the lakehouse, surprised to see that no car was there. "I could've sworn she'd be here," Gavin said angrily, slamming his fists into the steering wheel and beginning to turn the car around.

"Wait!" Gunner cried, his phone ringing in his pocket. It was Reagan. His heart leapt. "Hello?" he called into it.

It was mostly static, but he could hear what sounded like Nora crying in the background.

"Nora? Reagan?" He put it on speaker phone.

"Gun—?" He heard her panicked voice. "Gunner? Can—me?"

"Hello? Reagan?" he screamed, pressing the phone's volume button up as loud as it would go. "I'm here. I can hear you."

"Can—hear—Gun—car—ake." Her voice came in short bursts.

"We don't have enough service," Gunner yelled. "Damnit. Reagan, hold on, baby. I'm here. I'm here. I'm trying to get where I can hear you." He looked to Gavin. "Get me somewhere where I have service!"

Gavin did as he was instructed, driving back down the long, dusty driveway as quickly as he could. They could hear the police sirens headed their way. "Are you still there, Rae?"

"Car—own—die—ear me?"

"Keep talking, Rae. I'm getting closer to getting service. Keep talking to me."

"Love—ou—ease—car—ake—oat—she's gone!"

"Stop!" He screamed as soon as her voice came through clearly. "Can you hear me? Did you say she's gone?"

"Can you—me?" she asked hysterically.

"Yes!" he cried. "Where are you?" Tears rushed to his eyes at hearing her voice. She was still alive.

"We're—car, Gunner—the lake. We're go—drown. Sh—eft on a boat—pushed the car—lake. It's filli—water. We can't —doors open—tied up. I don't know what—do. Please, Gun—lease do somethi—"

He looked behind them. "I'm here, Reagan. Where are you? I'm here. I'm at the lake. I'm coming for you."

He could hear their cries coming through the phone. "Reagan, calm down. I need you to talk to me so I can find you. The police are on their way. Where are you?"

"I—I don't—ow. Not far from—gra—arents' house."

"Which way did she take you? North or south after you got to my grandparents'?"

"Right. We turned right," she answered, the answer clear.

Gavin had already turned the car back around. When they pulled back into the driveway, Gunner broke out of the car in a dead run, his legs getting ahead of him. He held the phone up, though her voice had begun cutting out terribly again.

"Ple—urry!"

"I'm hurrying!" he swore to her just as the line beeped, signaling to him that the call had dropped.

He ran behind their house, scanning the shoreline. The car was nowhere to be seen. He ducked through the trees, hearing Gavin hurrying behind him but he couldn't be bothered to slow down. He ran through the woods, limbs and weeds smacking him as he went. Blood trickled down his face from a particularly nasty branch, but he didn't wipe it away. All that mattered was getting to them. He ran, his legs carrying him long past when he thought they would give out.

Finally, he saw it—the black car sinking into the dark water of the lake. He sucked in a breath, jumping into the cool water. The car was nearly submerged, but he could see their heads peeking up for their last bit of air. He swam to it, water lapping and smacking at his face with vengeance. When he reached the car, he pulled on the door handle, the weight of the vehicle pulling him down rapidly as it sank. They had only seconds left. He screamed, beating on the windows with all of his might. He swam around to the front of the car, climbing onto the hood, and causing the car to sink faster. He cursed as water filled his mouth and he shoved all of his weight onto the glass. It didn't budge. Suddenly, Gavin was at his side, a large stone in his hands. He struggled to keep it above water as they both kicked and flailed.

They can't die. They can't die. The phrase repeated over and over in his head as they pounded the stone onto the window to no avail. As a last resort, Gunner swam around to the back of the car. "Help me try again," he screamed. Gavin did as he was told without comment, swimming around to him. They took the rock, holding it high above their heads and smacking it onto the only visible part of the back windshield. He realized he was going to watch them die just as soon as the window began to crack. They smacked it again, knocking out a bit more of the glass. Understanding he had less than thirty seconds before they would both be dead, he forced himself into the car, ignoring the glass of the windshield as it ripped his sides open.

The car still had a slight pocket of air and he took a deep breath before submerging and feeling for their bodies. He couldn't see anything in the dark water. He felt Reagan's hand shoving Nora into his and he pushed up out of the seat, forcing the girl to the top. He heard her catch a breath, music to his ears, and pushed her out of the window where Gavin was waiting. Without a pause, he went back down, grabbing at Reagan. He pulled her up but was immediately pulled down. He felt his way down her body, realizing she was tied to the tethers under the seat. He pulled at them with little force, the water working against him. Finally, he reached in his back pocket, pulling out a pocket knife and attempting to sever the ties, fearing he may cut her. Within seconds, she was free and he felt her legs kick off of the floorboard. She bounded up, banging her head on the roof of the car. There was no air pocket this time. He shoved with all of his might, hearing the back windshield giving way as she went through it. The water surrounded him entirely and his lungs burned as he climbed out of the windshield, desperate for air. Nora could be seen back on the shore, laying down, unmoving. Gavin was fighting the current with Reagan in his arms. Gunner felt defeated, his body sore, bleeding, and exhausted, but he kicked off the trunk making a last ditch effort to get out of the water. He swam, his arms and legs burning and begging for relief, though they continued moving. He could see the flashing lights telling him the police had arrived. The murky water splashed into his face relentlessly; he tasted it, blinked it into his eyes.

Finally, when he'd reached the shore, he collapsed next to the three others, panting heavily. He clutched his chest, watching his hand move up and down as his lungs screamed for air. He touched the sores on his sides, looking at his blood-covered hand. A police officer approached him.

"Sir, can you hear me?" she asked.

"Yes," he answered, his breathing increasingly more difficult.

"We're going to get you some help," she promised him.

He looked over at Reagan and Nora, noticing they weren't moving. "Are they okay?" he demanded.

An officer stood over Reagan. "We need a bus out here," he demanded into the radio on his shoulder.

"Everyone's alive," the cop assured Gunner. "Just lay still. We're going to get you guys some help."

Beside him, Reagan opened her eyes and Gunner inched his way to her side, ignoring his own pain. "Are you okay?" he asked.

"Sir, you shouldn't be moving right now. You need to remain still until we can assess your injuries." The officer tried to lay him down flat, but he refused to budge.

She smiled at him, her eyes pure and full of love. Her voice was soft and raspy when she spoke. "Why are you always saving me, Gunner James?"

THIRTY-TWO

REAGAN

Reagan woke up in the hospital, staring into the blinding white light above her. She lay still, struggling to catch her breath. All around her, she could feel the dark water closing in. She could still picture the terrified look on Nora's face as she waited for her mother to save them before realizing that wasn't going to happen.

Gia had tied them both down, making sure they couldn't escape. Nora had managed to untie herself and one of Reagan's hands eventually, her wrists smaller than the rope could account for, but by that time the water had risen too much—making it impossible for the doors to be opened. Gia had made sure to tear off the handles that rolled the windows down before she left them, ensuring there would be no escape. She'd felt panic growing inside of her as the cool, brown water filled the car, soaking them. Already claustrophobic, the scenario was enough to make Reagan feel as though her heart may explode. But it hadn't. She'd forced herself to stay calm. To think. Nora had pulled Reagan's phone from her pants pocket once her own hands were free and, by some miracle, it still worked. Reagan instructed her to keep it above their heads. The screen was foggy—a sure sign of water damage already. Following Reagan's instructions carefully, she found Gunner's number and dialed.

When they realized Gunner couldn't hear them because of the horrible service, Reagan began to accept that Gia may have won. As the car drifted further out onto the lake, with less trees to block them, he seemed to be able to hear her better, but she still couldn't be sure. With her free arm, she'd pulled her daughter close, trying to keep her safe for as long as possible. As the water rose even further, she held Nora up so she was still in the air pocket, though Reagan herself wouldn't be able to stay above water for much longer.

When she'd finally seen Gunner, it was as if an angel had appeared to her. Her angel. She knew Gunner would save them—he always did. And so, as the water began to fill her mouth, covering her eyes and ears, she felt hopeful. As her lungs burned for air, she knew somehow, someway it would be okay. And then, she'd felt his arms on her, felt Nora leave her hands, and she knew she'd been right. Right about everything. All those years ago, she'd loved Gunner before he'd proven himself to her. She'd loved him because behind those dark, troubled eyes—she'd seen the real Gunner. The man who would save her life countless times. The man who would dance with her in the middle of an empty dance floor. The man who would make her laugh when no one else would. The man who would love her like no one else could.

He'd pulled her out of the car and she'd felt peace. If she survived this, it would be because she'd chosen to trust a boy she was never supposed to fall in love with. And yet, she had. Even after all these years, she couldn't deny how much she loved him. Because she did. She always had. Gunner James was the dark cloud in her too-light sky. He was the perfect amount of shade. Dark, dangerous, and safe all at once. He'd been meant for her, and she him. Nothing would ever change her mind about that. Not ever again.

Brought back to reality, the door to her room opened and Jesse rushed in, his face distraught.

"Oh my god," he said, scooping her up gently into his arms. "I came as soon as they called. Are you okay?" He kissed her face, her hair, tears filling his eyes.

"I'm okay," she told him, hugging him back.

"Oh, Rae, I was so worried. That flight here was the worst of my life. I was so scared I was going to lose you." He continued to look her over, rubbing his fingers over the stitches covering her arms, shoulders, and sides.

"I'm so sorry, Jesse," she said, tears filling her own eyes.

"What do you have to be sorry for?" he asked. "I'm just so glad you're safe." He pressed his lips onto hers. "Where's Nora? Is she okay?"

"She's okay," Reagan said softly, biting her lip. "She's resting now."

"I should go check on her," he said, starting to leave the room.

She squeezed his hand, not letting go. "Jesse, wait."

He turned to face her. "What is it, sweetheart?"

She frowned. "I'm sorry," she repeated.

He closed his eyes. "I know."

She cocked her head to the side as he walked closer to her. "You know?"

"It's Gunner, isn't it?" he asked.

She nodded, rubbing her hand over his face. "I love you so much."

"But you love him more?" he asked, though his face told her he already knew the answer.

She nodded, unable to speak. He touched her hair. "I know," he repeated. "I knew we were over the second he came back into town." He shrugged, a tear falling down his cheek. "A guy can hope he's wrong, right?"

She brushed the tear from his chin. "I wish it wasn't this way," she whispered. And she did. On paper, Jesse was the perfect guy for her. Smart, successful, kind. He'd been good to her, taken care of her and Nora when they'd needed it most. And yet, her heart was and always had been with Gunner.

"I do too," he told her. "I just want you to be happy. You know that, right?"

She wiped a tear from her eyes. "You're supposed to be mean to me. Tell me what a horrible person I am."

"Rae, you're far from a horrible person. The heart wants what it wants."

She pulled the diamond ring from her finger, handing it to him. "Here," she said softly.

He took it from her. "I did tell you I'm a doctor, right? Like uber-rich, can save your life kind of doctor? Pretty good-looking, too, from what I hear." He smiled at his own joke, attempting to look braver than she knew he felt.

"I've heard that somewhere," she said, laughing through her tears.

He pressed his lips into her forehead. “I’m so glad you’re okay.”

“I’m sorry, Jesse,” she said, because she could think of nothing else. “You deserve better than this.”

“Eh, we had a pretty good ride. You just promise me you’ll take care of yourself, okay? And tell Gunner I’ll be waiting for him to slip up.”

She smiled, letting go of his hand. “I will.”

“I’m going to go say goodbye to Nora,” he said, taking a step back.

“Okay,” she said, watching him slip the ring into his pocket. He turned around, opening the door and casting one last look her way before he disappeared out of it. She let out a broken sob, allowing herself to grieve the relationship she’d hung so much hope on. She shook, wrapping her arms around herself despite the pain. It would have been easier if he’d been a jerk about it, but she’d known better than that. That wasn’t the Jesse she knew.

A few more minutes passed before the door opened again. Her parents bustled into the room.

“How are you feeling?” her mother asked. Her father carried a few things from the cafeteria downstairs. He offered her a soda.

“No, thanks,” she said. “I’m okay. Still sore.”

“Do you want us to see if the nurse can give you some pain medicine?”

“She’s already given me some,” Reagan told them. “I’ll be okay.”

Her mother sat down in the seat beside her bed, grasping her hand. “We were just in to see Nora. Jesse seemed upset.”

Reagan nodded. “Mom, I—”

"Did you call off the engagement?" Gemma asked. She nodded again. Gemma sighed. "I figured that was what was going on."

"I'm sorry," Reagan said.

"What on earth are you apologizing to me for?" she asked, her eyes wide.

"I know you liked him. I know you thought he was good for us."

Her mother stroked her palm. "He is good for you, Rae. Jesse is a good man. But, the only thing truly good for you...is your own happiness. With Holly gone, you're all we have left." Tears brimmed her eyes. "You and Nora. And your happiness is all that matters to us. We want you safe. And happy. And loved. And cared for. And if you are all of those things, then I'm happy. I know what you and Gunner had was special. I may not like the way he treated you at the end, but the way he treats you now is what's truly important. I'm willing to forgive mistakes made nearly ten years ago, sweetheart. He saved your life."

"More than you know," Reagan said. "I love you."

Her mother placed her head down beside her daughter's. "I love you too, my sweet girl."

The door opened once more and Gunner was standing in the threshold, his skin pale. His hair had dried strangely, sticking out in every direction. "Oh," he said, "I'm sorry." He began to walk away, but Gemma stopped him.

"Come in here, Gunner."

He did as he was told, walking cautiously into the room and to Reagan's other side. "I can come back later," he told them.

"Nonsense," Scott said. "No reason for that."

Reagan reached up, taking his hand. "It's okay, Gunner. Everything's okay now." She ran her fingers along the bulk under his shirt where the bandages were. "Shouldn't you be in bed somewhere?"

"Just a few stitches," he said casually. "I wanted to check on you and Nora."

"We're both going to be fine," she said. "Thanks to you."

"You saved their lives, Gunner," Gemma said. "We can't thank you enough."

Scott reached out to shake his hand, seemingly unable to speak.

"I couldn't live without them," Gunner said. "So really, I was just saving my own."

Reagan pulled him down to her, kissing his hand. He sat. "We never want to live without you again."

Gemma took a breath. "Are you going to stay around here, then? Stay in Dale?"

He nodded. "I'm not going anywhere."

"Good." She seemed pleased with that answer. "I suppose we'll be seeing you around, then." She kissed Reagan's head.

"I suppose you will," Gunner agreed.

"We'll give you two some space," Gemma said, standing up.

"You don't have to go."

"We won't be gone too long," Scott said. "We'll just head over and check on Nora again."

They disappeared from the room. The second the door closed, Reagan pulled his face to hers, kissing him softly.

"I thought you wanted to wait."

"I talked to Jesse," she said.

"Already?" he asked, a smile on his face.

"I'm in a hurry to be in love with you, Gunner James. Officially."

He kissed her back, his hands cupping her face. "There was never a time when I wasn't in love with you, Reagan."

She squeezed his hand, her fingers on her own cheeks. "I've been waiting a very long time to hear you say that."

"I've been waiting a long time to be able to say it."

"Gunner, move in with me."

"Yes," he said instantly, not having to think twice.

"What? Seriously? I thought there would have to be some serious convincing done before you'd agree. That was too easy."

He shook his head, kissing her again. "We've already lost eight years. I love you. I love Nora. You never have to convince me of anything again. I'm in this. I'm with you. And I'm never, ever going anywhere."

THIRTY-THREE

GUNNER

The next week, Reagan was ready to come home from the hospital. Gunner paced the house. "Nora, are you ready to go?" he called. She walked out of her room.

"I'm ready!" she exclaimed. "Let's go get Mom."

As they walked out the door and climbed into the car, Gunner looked at her. "Now, remember what we talked about."

"No telling Mom about the ice cream for dinner...twice." She smiled at him devilishly.

"That's right." He smiled, starting up the car and backing out of the drive.

"Gunner?" the girl asked, once they were a bit further down the road.

"Yes?"

"Are you going to live with us forever?"

"Well," he said, "that's the plan. Is that okay with you?"

She thought for a moment before answering. "I think so."

He was shocked by her answer. "I thought you'd be excited."

"It's just always been me and Mommy. Things are going to be different now."

"Well, that's true," he agreed. "But different doesn't have to mean bad. Different can be really good."

"Like how?"

"Well, I guess that's up to you. Nothing you don't want to change has to change. You and your mom can still have all the time you want together. But I'll be there too, sometimes. And we can play games or watch movies or whatever dads and daughters do together."

"You're not very good at this whole dad thing, are you?" she asked skeptically.

"I haven't had much practice, Nora, if I'm being honest with you. I'm learning as I go. But...I want to learn to be a good dad for you. I think you deserve the best dad there is."

"Is that you?"

"I hope it will be someday."

"Me too," she told him.

"You know, being your dad is going to take me some time to get used to. And I may not always do the right things and sometimes you might not like me all that much but I'm always going to try my hardest for you."

"I'll help you." She smiled at him.

"I'd like that a lot." He felt the lump growing in his throat.

"You said I can call you Dad, but is it okay if I just keep calling you Gunner...for now?"

"You can call me whatever you want. Just don't call me late for dinner."

She stared at him. "What?"

He laughed to himself. "Nothing. It was a joke I've heard other dads make. I think I'm supposed to make corny jokes now or something."

She furrowed her brow. "I don't get it."

"That's okay, kiddo. I never really did either."

She patted her legs, looking out the window. "There's a father-daughter dance at school coming up."

"Oh yeah?" he said.

"Jesse was supposed to take me."

"Well, that would be all right."

"But he's not really my father, is he?"

"Not really, no. But that doesn't mean he can't take you," Gunner said, feeling pain at her words.

"Most of the kids...their real fathers take them."

"Do you want me to take you?" he offered.

"Do you think that would be okay?"

"We could ask Jesse what he thinks," Gunner said. "Maybe we could both take you."

"There's a kid in my class who has two dads."

"People have families that come all kinds of different ways."

"I like our family," she said finally, wrapping a hand around his arm.

He smiled at her, staring down at her wide, innocent eyes with nothing but love. "I like our family, too."

AS THEY WALKED down the halls in the hospital, Nora counted the numbers on the doors. "Three hundred two, three hundred four, three hundred six, three hundred eight."

Gunner pulled her to a stop as the door to one opened and he saw a familiar face.

"What is it?" Nora asked, looking into the room. Misty wasn't someone she'd recognize and Gunner had no plans of changing that.

"Um, nothing, here's the elevator. Come on." He let her press the button and they walked onto it quickly.

"Who was that old lady?" she asked as the elevator began to rise.

"Just someone who's sick, sweetie."

"Did you know her?"

"Nope, I thought I did, but I was wrong."

The doors opened again and they were on Reagan's floor. "Mommy!" Nora cried, seeing her mother standing just beyond the open doorway, talking to a doctor. She smiled up at them, holding her arms out for Nora.

Gunner pointed at the elevator. *I'll be right back,* he mouthed the words, holding up a finger. Reagan looked confused, but nodded anyway.

He climbed back on before the doors shut and pressed number three. He was back in her doorway within minutes.

He walked in without knocking. She lay in bed, a thin gown covering her frail body. An oxygen mask had been placed over her nose and mouth. Her bandana was missing, revealing a mostly bare scalp.

Her wild eyes found him. She reached for the mask slowly, pulling it down. "Gunner, my boy," she croaked. The cancer was killing her rapidly, it was evident.

"Misty," he said formally.

"Misty? Since when do you call me..." She placed the mask to her mouth, taking a breath before she could speak again. "Misty?"

"Since you quit being my mother." She shook her head, the mask pressed to her mouth. "All those years, I tried to protect you. Protect them. I hated my father...but all along, you were the only monster under that roof. You were the one I should've hated."

She shook her head again.

"How could you do that? How could you hurt them? What did they ever do to you?"

"Your father...was..." She took a breath and removed the mask. "...a cheater."

"So were you," he said indignantly.

"I wish..." she croaked. "That...was...the lie I told...him...to...get even."

"What are you talking about?"

"He had an affair...when I was...pregnant with you...the bastard."

"So you had an affair to get even?"

"I never...had...an affair...it was...a lie."

"You lied about your affair?"

"To...hurt...him...like he hurt...me." Her chest was rising and falling heavily, a monitor beginning to beep faster.

"So, Gavin and Gia were his kids all along?"

She nodded, sucking down the oxygen.

"You lied to all of us for years? Just to make yourself feel better?"

She sucked in another breath. "Screw...him...." she whispered, a small smile in her eyes.

"You're sick, you know that? You ruined all of our lives. You ruined your families' lives for some sick vendetta. And look where it got you, where it got us: he's dead, Gavin's on the run, Gia's seriously screwed up, and I've spent years away from the only true family I've ever had. All because you're selfish. And evil."

"I…did…what I had to."

"Now, I'm going to do what I have to." The voice came from behind him. He looked up to see Gavin walking toward them. Misty smiled.

"Back…again?" she asked him.

"I'm done running. You started the fire. You tried to kill your children. You abused us all those years. You're to blame for everything."

"I never…started the fire."

"Well, that doesn't matter," he said, walking up beside of Gunner. "Because after today, that's what people are going to believe. See, I'm done lying for you, Misty, and I'm done hiding. I'm done. Gunner didn't see all the horrible shit you did to us. How you burned us, broke our fingers, punched our faces, cut Gia's hair, called her names, starved her. You were cruel to me, but Gia always got it the worst. Were you jealous of her? Was that it? You hated her the most, but I never knew why. You were good at hiding. Good at lying. My sister was a good person at one point, but she had no choice with you. She had no choice but to become who she is now. And that's on you. But I'll be damned if I don't find her and make sure she gets the help she needs. And that can't happen if you're still alive."

He grabbed the oxygen mask, pulling it off of her. She grasped for it, clawing and scratching his hands, her nails drawing blood. For a moment, Gunner stood, watching, but he had to stop it. Not for her, but for his brother. He couldn't let his life be ruined any more.

"Gavin, stop," he told him, trying to grab the oxygen mask from his hand.

"No, Gunner, you don't understand. You don't know what she's done. You didn't have to live it." He was crying, his words coming out in sobs.

"If you do this, she still wins. She still controls you. The only way to be truly free is to walk away right now. She's dying anyway. She's going to die soon. But if you kill her, that will stay with you for the rest of your life. You see what killing has done to Gia. It destroyed her, man. Don't let it happen to you, too. I'll back you up. I'll help protect you. Help get Gia the help she needs. But you have to stop." Gunner pleaded with his brother, trying desperately to get him to look at him. "Don't let Misty control one more thing in your life."

With that, Gavin thrust the oxygen back into her hands. "She doesn't deserve to live," he said firmly, walking away and out of the room as Misty's breathless, evil cackles echoed behind him.

"You think you've won," Gunner said, "but the truth is...we win. We win because we get to keep on living. But you, you're done here. You may have another week or maybe a month, but this is all of the life you have. You're alone, Misty. You're going to die alone." Without another word, he strolled from the room, wanting nothing more than to see his family.

THIRTY-FOUR

GUNNER

When they got home, Gunner helped Reagan from the car. "I'm okay," she told him. "Honestly, I am."

He backed up, still staying close beside her. He opened the door, setting her bag down. "Are you hungry?" he asked. "I can make you something to eat."

"We just ate lunch half an hour ago, Gun," she assured him. "I'm okay. The doctor said I should resume normal activity."

"The doctor also said you should take it easy."

"I appreciate you worrying. But, really, I just need to change out of these clothes and take a shower."

The doorbell rang behind him and Nora rushed to get it. "Nora, what did your mother tell you about—" Gunner began to scold her.

"Grandma and Grandpa!" she yelled, jumping into their waiting arms.

"Hello, my sweet," Gemma kissed her on the head.

"Mom, Dad, what are you doing here?" Reagan asked, hugging them both slowly, trying to hide her pain.

"We came to see if Nora wanted to spend the night with us. That way you can get settled in."

"You don't have to take her," Reagan said. "I'm not sure I'm ready to be away from her again."

"She'll be fine. We've missed her too, you know," Gemma said.

"Please can I go, Mommy? Please?" Nora begged.

"You don't want to stay home with Mommy?" Reagan asked, pretending to pout.

"Grandma and Grandpa let me have brownies," she said, rubbing her hands together as if she had an evil plot.

"They do, do they?" Reagan raised her eyebrows.

"You weren't supposed to tell that." Gemma touched her forehead to the girl's. "That was our secret."

The girl shrugged. "There's too many secrets."

"Are there more?" Reagan asked.

"Don't look in the trash!" Nora giggled.

"Have you been feeding my child sugar?" Reagan teased Gunner.

"I was coerced, I swear." He ruffled Nora's hair playfully.

"Oh, fine, Grandma and Grandpa are cooler than Mommy," Reagan said, giving in.

"Not cooler, Mommy. Just a little sweeter," Nora said, leaning from her grandmother's arms to kiss Reagan.

"Go get your bags packed, little missy." Gemma patted her bottom.

Nora ran from the room, returning a few seconds later with a bag.

"You've got everything you need? Toothbrush, hairbrush, pajamas, socks, underwear, clothes?" Reagan recited the list.

"Yep, I've got everything!" she exclaimed.

"All right, give me a kiss, then." She kissed her daughter. "I love you."

Nora walked to stand in front of Gunner. He bent down. "Have fun," he told her.

"Take care of my mommy," she instructed, wagging her finger at him.

He held out a pinky. "Pinky swear."

Her eyes lit up. "You know about pinky swears?"

"I know a thing or two."

She threw her arms around his neck. "I love you, Gunner."

"I love you too, Nor," he said, rubbing her back.

With that, they were off. "Take care of her." Reagan and Gunner waved to them as they pulled down the street. Once they were gone, Gunner shut the door.

"Are you okay?" he asked.

"I'm better than okay," she said, wrapping her arms around his neck and kissing him. He fell into her kiss, his arms surrounding her waist, minding her bandages.

"I missed you," he said.

"I've been missing you for a very long time."

"Oh yeah?" he asked, pushing her back into the wall.

"Yeah," she whispered breathlessly.

"Never again," he said.

"Never," she agreed.

His lips found hers again, his skin suddenly on fire for

her. He lifted her shirt over her head carefully, revealing the gauze that ran down her sides. "Is this okay?" he asked.

"You don't have to ask that anymore," she said, pulling his off as well.

"I don't want to hurt you."

She grabbed his hand, pulling him down the hall. "You won't." They entered her bedroom, shutting the door behind them. She attempted to pull her bra off but winced and stopped.

"Here," he said, "let me." He moved slowly, his hands finding the clasp. His face was next to hers, his lips on her ear. "We don't have to rush."

"I've been waiting for you, for this, for eight years." Her hands found his pants and she undid the button quickly, pulling them down.

"I don't have protection," he told her.

She reached into the dresser drawer, pulling a condom out. "Not that it helped us much last time." He tried to ignore the fact that this particular condom had probably once been meant for Jesse. She kissed him, his passion growing as she walked him backward toward the bed. He sat. His hands moved to her pants and he slid them carefully over her legs, pulling her onto the bed. His hands cupped her breasts, his mouth running over them. "You're so beautiful," he whispered.

She pulled him close to her, taking the condom from his hands, tearing open the package and sliding it over him. He was ready. He rolled over so he was on top of her, staring down in amazement. He slid inside of her as she let out a shocked moan.

She gripped his back, pushing him into her harder, her

face buried in his shoulder. He kissed the side of her head, putting his weight on one arm so he could hold the back of her head. Her body moved rhythmically with his, their breaths heavy.

"I love you," she said. He felt cool tears gathering on his bare skin and he stopped moving, looking at her.

"Is it your stitches? Are you hurting?"

"No," she whispered, "it's my heart. It's finally *stopped* hurting."

He sank into her again, his mouth meeting hers. *Mine too*, he thought, *mine too.*

THIRTY-FIVE

GUNNER
TWO MONTHS LATER

"Where are we going?" Reagan asked again.

"Patience, grasshopper," Gunner taunted. Beside him, Nora snickered, covering her mouth.

He led her to the edge of the black pavement, staring at the large white building. "Open your eyes," he whispered in her ear.

She moved her hands from her eyes and gasped instantly, her face lighting up at the sight of the large helicopter. "You remembered?" She squealed, covering her mouth and jumping up and down.

"You don't forget something as crazy as that," he said, laughing. "Now, you don't actually get to fly today. Nora and I wanted to go with you and lessons only allow you and the instructor to go up. But I figured this would be a good starting point and then, if you want, you can take the course."

"I'm going to learn to fly a helicopter?" she asked excitedly.

"You're going to learn to fly a helicopter." His happiness grew, realizing how much this meant to her.

She grabbed Nora's hand, running to where the pilot was waiting for them. He handed them helmets and began explaining how everything worked. Reagan was hardly listening, her over-the-moon excitement completely evident. He told them all where they should sit so the weight would be distributed evenly and helped them to get strapped in. The cockpit was almost entirely made of glass and much to Gunner's surprise the doors were shut, closing them in. Action movies had done so little to prepare him for this.

Reagan reached over Nora, squeezing Gunner's hand. "Are you excited?" she asked Nora, a bit too loudly, into the microphone. Nora nodded, though she looked a bit nervous.

The pilot began talking, asking for clearance, and pretty soon the blades above them began to whirl. They were extremely loud, even inside the aircraft, and Gunner suddenly understood why the headsets were necessary.

"All right, folks, here we go," the pilot said as the aircraft began lifting up. There was no runway, in fact, it felt more like an elevator than anything as it lifted straight into the air. Gunner's stomach lurched just a bit as he stared out over Atlanta, the sun gleaming off the tall buildings. He looked over, no matter how beautiful the city was, it couldn't come close to the sight of his girls looking out the window, their eyes wide with pure joy. Reagan looked back at him, her smile wide.

"It's amazing," she said.

"Yes, it is," he agreed.

The pilot told them what they were seeing, pointing out a few landmarks here and there. For the most part, Gunner wasn't listening. He couldn't take his eyes off Reagan, who looked like a two-year-old on Christmas morning. Everything was more magical through her eyes. He rubbed Nora's shoulder, grinning as her smile grew.

"This is awesome," she told him, giving him a hug. "Best surprise ever."

"I'm glad you think so."

Once they'd made their trip around the city, the pilot let them know they would be headed back. There was a bit of turbulence as the helicopter found its way to the ground and Nora squeezed his arm. "We're okay," he assured her.

She nodded, though she didn't let go. As they made their way out of the helicopter, Reagan was still gushing. "Thank you," she told the pilot as she handed back her helmet.

"So, what did you think?" Gunner asked.

"Oh, Gunner, that was the most amazing thing I've ever done. I can't believe you set that up for me."

He smiled. "It was fun. Number one thing on your bucket list? Check!" He made the 'checkmark' motion with his hand in the air, throwing an arm around her shoulder.

"No," she said.

"Okay, well, not technically, because you didn't learn to fly it yet. But we can go right in here and pay for your lessons so you can learn. I just wanted to make sure you loved it as much as you thought you would."

"No," she said again, turning to face him. "I mean, that isn't number one on my bucket list. Not anymore."

"No?" He cocked his head to the side. "What's number one, then? Are we moving on to submarines now? 'Cause I don't know if I can swing that." He smiled at her playfully.

"Becoming your wife."

He gulped. "Wait, what?"

"Marry me, Gunner." She stared at him, her face stoic. "Marry me."

"What?" he repeated.

"I know it's soon. Too soon. But, I mean…is it really? We're like ten years in the making with a slight break in there, right? I'm tired of waiting. I'm tired of hoping. We've wasted too much time. I love you and you love me, so why wait anymore? Right? Let's do this thing, Gunner. Like, for real. Let's be all in. You and me."

"And me!" Nora interjected.

"And her," she said, her eyebrows raised as she let out a laugh. "So, say yes, Gun. Say yes and marry me already."

"No," he said.

"No?"

"You aren't supposed to ask me." He reached into his pocket, pulling out a ring box. "I was going to ask you. Tonight."

"Oh, no," she said, covering her mouth. "Well, I asked you first. And you said yes."

"I haven't said yes."

She took the ring box from him and slid the diamond band over her finger, kissing his lips with a full smile still on her face. "You said yes. And that's the story we're telling the grandkids. Face it, mister, you were too slow. Momma had to make the first move."

He pulled her into another kiss, a smile growing on his own face. “Whatever you say.”

“He said yes!” Nora screamed. “She said yes! They said yes!” A few people nearby clapped, laughing and congratulating them as they passed. “So when will you get married? Tomorrow?”

“No, Nora, not tomorrow,” Reagan said, bending down to hug her daughter. “But soon.”

Gunner bent down beside them. “Very soon.”

Reagan seemed impressed. “Very soon, hm?”

“It’s like you said...no more waiting.”

THIRTY-SIX

REAGAN

FOUR MONTHS LATER

Reagan walked into Gunner's dressing room. "We're officially white-trash," she told him exasperatedly.

He took a step back, his eyes taking her in. She was more breathtaking than usual on that particular day. "I thought I wasn't supposed to see you in your dress."

She waved her hand. "Ah, we've already had all the bad luck. We survived it." She sank down in a chair.

"Well, in that case, you look beautiful." He walked over, hugging her as he sank to his knees in front of her, his hands resting in her lap.

She began tying the tie he'd been struggling with. "Thank you. You don't look so bad yourself."

He ran his hands over the tie, checking it once she was done. "Are you doubting my handiwork?" she accused him joyfully.

"Never," he said, kissing her forehead. "Just double checking it. Now, what were you saying about us being...what was it?"

"White-trash. You know, like...shotgun weddings."

"Shotgun weddings?" His eyes grew wide. "You're pregnant?"

She nodded, biting her lip. "Bad timing?" she asked. "I found out this morning. I couldn't stand being the only one who knew."

It wasn't in the plan. Not yet. "Are you excited?"

She smiled, nodding apprehensively. "I kind of am."

He laughed, his chest swelling with pride. "We have got to stop using that brand of condoms," he joked.

"Our babies just really want to be made, Mr. James," she said, brushing the hair back from his eyes.

"Well, we do make really, really awesome babies, Mrs. James." He leaned in to kiss her.

She leaned back, wagging her finger. "Ah, ah, ah, not just yet. We still have..." She glanced at her wrist as if she were wearing a watch. "About thirty minutes before we make it official. One last chance for you to run." She winked.

"Or..." He smiled fiendishly, making her face flush. "I could think of something else we could do with that thirty minutes."

She laughed loudly. "Me too. Milkshakes."

"That wasn't exactly what I had in mind. Cravings already?" He smirked.

"Hey, you missed out on all the first cravings. I'm milking this one for everything it's worth."

He scratched his chin. "Think we can make a fast getaway?"

She stood up, pulling him to his feet. "Oh, the thing every woman hopes to hear on her wedding day." They walked to the door and she stopped, pulling off her heels and darting down the steps, with him following close behind. They laughed loudly in spite of themselves. Gunner felt more free than he'd felt in so long. Everything was right in his life. Finally, he felt like things were actually going to be okay. He climbed into the car, helping her pull her dress in before she shut the door and they drove away.

Within minutes, they were at a local diner. "Chocolate?" Gunner asked, opening his door.

She nodded. "Hurry, I have this nagging feeling we're running late for something." She flashed a smile at him.

He ran into the building, approaching the counter. "Can I get two milkshakes, please?" he asked, looking around the empty building.

A man walked up from the back and Gunner gasped. "Gavin?"

"Gunner? What—" He stared at his tux. "What are you wearing?"

"I'm...uh, I'm getting married today." He touched his tie.

"What?" He seemed shocked, looking away. "Um, well, congratulations, man."

"Thank you," Gunner said.

"Uh, so, milkshakes, you said? What kind?"

"Oh, right, yeah. One chocolate and one banana."

He began working on the shakes, talking over the machine. "What brought you to Atlanta?"

"We, uh, Reagan is taking flying lessons here. We're getting married at a church she loves to look at when she flies over the city."

"Reagan, huh? I should have known."

"Yeah." Gunner rubbed the back of his neck, feeling tense.

"Well, congrats again." He scooped a banana into a glass blender, pouring milk into it.

"What brought you here?"

"Just wanted to get away from all the bad stuff, you know? Atlanta wasn't far. Plus, Gia's here. I'm keeping tabs on her."

"Oh, so, you've heard from Gia?"

"She's in a facility here in town. Under a fake name. I sort of convinced them she is delusional. It wasn't too hard with her claiming to be a dead girl and all. I'm just...I'm scared of what will happen if they know the truth." His face was grim. "Anyway, I'm doing what I can to keep her there. It's a good place. She's trying to work through some stuff, you know? I guess we both are. I go and visit her every once in a while. Maybe you could go with me sometime."

"Yeah, maybe," Gunner said, though he knew he never would. Gia had taken Reagan's sister away. He wasn't sure he could ever forgive her for that.

"Well, anyway, good luck with everything," Gavin said, setting the milkshakes in front of him.

"Thanks. How much do I owe you?"

Gavin waved his hand. "Nothing. It's on the house."

"No, let me pay." Gunner held out a ten dollar bill.

"Consider it my wedding present to you guys. And my apology. For whatever that's worth."

Gunner grabbed the milkshakes. "Thanks," he said awkwardly, walking to the door. He stopped just before he pushed it open. "Hey, Gav?"

Gavin looked at him, a glimmer of hope in his tired, dark eyes.

"I don't have a best man."

Gavin didn't need him to say anything further. He pushed the counter's door open and ran to Gunner, yelling over his shoulder. "I'm going on break." No one responded, but Gavin didn't seem to care.

He walked to the car and Gunner saw Reagan's confused look. She pressed the button to unlock the doors and Gavin climbed into the back. "Hey," he said quietly. "Is this okay?"

She looked to Gunner, who handed her a milkshake. "His gift to us," he said simply.

She took a sip. "This is amazing." She cast a small smile to Gavin in the backseat.

"Reagan, I'm—"

"Gunner told me you helped save my life," she interrupted him. "So, whatever you're planning to say, don't worry about it. Just know that you're forgiven."

"It's not that easy."

"I'm making it that easy, Gavin. It's my wedding day. And I'm choosing to be happy."

Gunner pulled out of the diner's parking lot and back into the church within minutes. They raced in, slurping down the last of their shakes and tossing the cups into the trash. She gave him one last kiss before she walked away.

"I'll see you at the end of the aisle," he told her.

"I'll be the one in white...with maybe a little bit of chocolate milkshake on my front." She gasped, glancing down with a horrified look on her face as she realized she had spilled her shake on the skirt of her dress.

"Come with me," Gunner said, taking her hand. "They can wait a little while longer."

"If we make them wait too much longer, we won't have any guests left."

"We're paying the priest. He's all we really need." He pulled her into a bathroom, turning on the faucet. "I can clean this for you."

"Well, silly me, I forgot I'm marrying a cleaner," she said, feigning surprise.

"Okay, that joke is going to get very old very fast." He scrubbed the warm water onto the dress carefully, watching the stain fade.

"Just as long as you promise to get old right along with it. Right by my side."

He stood up, satisfied with the faded stain. "I can't imagine anything else."

She looked down at where the chocolate had been and sighed, a smile growing on her face.

"Go ahead," he whispered. "Say it."

"Say what?" she asked.

"Your line."

"I have a line?" she asked, an eyebrow raised.

"Yeah...I think it goes something like—"

She winked at him, interrupting his sentence with a kiss, a kiss like the ones he hoped to experience every day for the rest of his life. A kiss so full of love and hope that nothing—not his family, his past, or his unending darkness—could ever diminish it. A kiss that said everything he wanted to say to her. How, even though she thought he'd been saving her all those years, it had really been her keeping him afloat. Reagan Orrick had saved his life more times than he could count.

And she would keep on saving him every day that she continued to love him.

"Why are you always saving me, Gunner James?"

"Because you are *so* worth saving, Reagan James."

Keep reading for a SNEAK PEEK of:

The Healer: The Messes Series #2

CHAPTER ONE

JESSE

"Time of death, twenty-two forty-five." Jesse Mathis stepped back from the operating table, pulling down the paper mask from his mouth and heaving a sigh. Cool tears collected in his eyes but he blinked them away, pulling the bloody gloves from his hands.

Her blood was all around him, on his surgical gown, beneath his feet. He could feel small specks of it drying on his face.

"Close her up, Donovan," he told the intern across from him. He nodded, his face solemn. Jesse wondered briefly if it was the first patient Donovan had lost. He couldn't remember. Or he didn't know. It didn't matter—they all hurt the same.

He stepped back through the heavy door, unable to catch his breath.

"Jesse?" Quinn's voice rang out from behind him, the

concern there as it so often was, but he didn't turn around. He couldn't. If he saw her face he would lose what little resolve he had left.

He ripped the gown off from his chest, tossing it into the biohazard bin and ran his hands under the faucet, waiting for the water to come on. When it did, he began scrubbing his hands. He cursed out loud, slamming his hands onto either side of the stainless steel wash basin.

The patient had been a mother. She had two teenage daughters he'd met earlier that evening. It was a simple surgery, a routine appendectomy. He hadn't been counting on the unexpected mass in her cecum. They hadn't seen it in her scans. The tissue was inflamed and needed a resection in order to prevent an impending small bowel obstruction. The hemorrhage wasn't his fault. If he'd known about the issue beforehand, he could've had time to prepare a plan.

But, she was gone. And his hands had been the ones meant to save her. He scrubbed harder, until his fingers were red, raw, and nearly bleeding. A small tear fell from his eyes and he wiped it away with his arm just as the door opened again.

The patient had been closed up. The surgery was over. As the nurses began filing out, each avoiding his eye contact, he stared into the operating room, looking at the blood that still coated the floor, the blue sheet that now covered her face. Quinn left the room last, touching his arm. When he looked at her, her eyes were grim.

"You didn't know," she said.

It didn't matter. "I should have."

"You couldn't have. Her family didn't know. Her doctor didn't know. It's not your fault."

He pulled away from her grasp. "I have to go tell her family. They'll be waiting for news."

She was calm as ever, closing her eyes and taking a breath. She spoke in a low, throaty tone. "Take a moment, Jess," she warned. "Pull yourself together first."

He shook off his hands over the sink, running his palms down his face and taking a deep breath. She patted his shoulder as she walked past him. He nodded toward her, thankful for her words. She smiled sadly, her eyes kind.

The conversation that was coming was the worst part of his job. He'd take draining a thousand pus-filled lesions over just the one conversation. The one where he had to tell her family that his hands had been the only thing between her and death, and no matter how hard he had tried—he couldn't save her.

Lately, that seemed to be a pattern for him. Losing people, both patients and fiancées. He walked down the hall, trying to clear his head and drain the emotion from his body. He couldn't allow himself to feel when he spoke to them. He had to be empty.

He passed through the double doors, entering the waiting room, his scrub cap in hand. Her husband saw him immediately, his worried eyes growing wide as he stood. He read the look on Jesse's face before he spoke.

"No," he said, shaking his head as his face began to scrunch up. His sobs tore through the quiet, too-cold room. "No," he repeated. Beside him, the girls stood up, their smiling faces fading. They fell into each other's arms before Jesse could speak the first word.

"I'm so sorry," he told them, though they were no longer looking his direction. The husband, a husky fellow with a balding head sank into a chair, his body shaking. "Evelyn didn't make it through surgery." He spoke over their sobs, needing to say it out loud. "When we began, I ran into a problem. Your wife had a mass in her abdomen, which was causing a slight blockage of her lower intestine. She needed a resection, but she started to hemorrhage. We gave her two pints of blood, but her blood pressure kept dropping. Her heart was having to work too hard. My team and I did all that we could to save her, but I'm afraid we weren't able to." He paused, fiddling with the calluses on his palms. "Your wife is dead, Mr. Ramirez." He closed his eyes, taking a breath. It was required that they use the word: dead. Not *passed away*, not *gone on*, not *no longer with us*. It was imperative that the family understood completely, though the word always felt harsh when spoken.

He stood for a few moments, watching them cry, before the eldest daughter looked up to him. "Can we, um," she paused, wiping her eyes with shaking hands, "can we see her?"

He nodded. "Yes, of course. They're getting her ready for you now. In just a few moments, a nurse will be able to take you back."

"I don't understand," the husband said, "it was just a simple surgery. The other doctor told us there was nothing to worry about."

"Dr. Sloane never should have told you that. I'm sorry he did. With surgery, there is always risk." His response was automatic–programmed in him like a script.

"You said a mass...what is that? Like a tumor? Why didn't they find that before the surgery? How long had it been there?"

"It's possible that it was a tumor, though that doesn't mean it was cancer. It could certainly have been benign, but without a biopsy, I can't say for sure. As for why we didn't know about the mass, it's difficult to say why it didn't show up on her scans, but it was likely causing her no symptoms quite yet."

The man nodded, blinking his eyes through heavy tears.

"Would you like me to give you a moment?"

Again, the man nodded, leaning onto his daughter's shoulder. Jesse took a step back, relief filling him. He turned around, heading out of the waiting room. He didn't belong there anymore. As he passed through the double doors again, he felt a weight leave his chest, his breath filling his lungs completely again. It was over. He'd done his part. Soon, one of the nurses would be along to check on them. Maybe Quinn. She was good at that—consoling the broken. He knew because she'd done it so often with him.

"Are you planning to come over tonight?" Quinn asked as they walked out of the locker room.

"Nah, I think I'll just head home."

"What? You're breaking tradition on me?"

"Yeah." He shrugged. "I just want to catch up on some sleep."

"Okay," she said, her eyes dancing between his, her brow low. "But...you're okay, right?"

"I'm fine, Q," he assured her, bowing his head. "I just need...I don't know...I just need a minute." They passed through the entrance to the hospital and out into the parking lot.

"Okay," she said, giving in, "but just don't go off and sulk alone. If you need something you'd better call me."

"I will."

She turned to walk away, jingling her keys over her head. "I'll see you tomorrow, right?"

"Tomorrow?" he asked, but the realization hit him as soon as he spoke. He opened his mouth again but no words came out. *Tomorrow. Reagan's wedding.*

"Are you sure you're—"

"Yeah, yep. Sorry, I just lost track of the day. I'll be there." "You're picking me up, right?"

He nodded. "I'll be there around noon."

She smiled. "See you then."

He turned away from her, walking the opposite direction to his car. The fact that his ex-fiancée's wedding was tomorrow made his already miserable night one million times worse.

As he climbed into his car and pulled out of the parking lot, he headed right, rather than left. He wasn't going home, not alone and not tonight.

LOVED THE CLEANER?

Thank you so much for reading The Cleaner! If you enjoyed Gunner and Reagan's story, I would love for you to check out the rest of the series!

The Healer—Jesse's story
The Liar—Fletcher's story
The Prisoner—Fiona's story

It is super important that the rest of the series is read in order! It's a wild ride...I hope you enjoy it!

If you do, I humbly ask that you consider leaving me a review on whatever platform you purchased this copy. It would truly mean the world to me.

XO,
Kiersten Modglin

ACKNOWLEDGMENTS

First and foremost, to *my husband and daughter*, for always supporting me, always loving me, and always forgiving me when my writing takes over our day. You guys are my driving force. I couldn't do any of this without you. I love you back.

To the rest of *my family*: thank you for continuing to read my stories and for believing in me. I don't know where I'd be without you guys and I never want to find out.

To *my PA Brittany*: you are my cheerleader, my beta reader, the person who talks me down from the cliff when I'm ready to quit, and my favorite partner. I am so glad I found you. You have helped me so much more than you know and I plan on keeping you around for as long as you'll have me!

To *my Twisted Readers*: you guys are amazing. Seriously. I don't know what I would do without our group. You keep me going, you lift me up when I'm having a bad day, and you keep me writing even when I really, really just want to go to bed. (HAHA!) I appreciate each and every one of you more than you know.

To *my Street Team*: ya'll are the best! I am so lucky to have you in my corner. Thank you for helping to share my work with the world. I am forever humbled by how much faith you have in me.

To the amazing ladies who share my work with the world daily and ask for nothing in return: Holly, Misty, Sarah, Joy, Janise, Gwen, Gemma, Crystal, Shelly, Alma, Danielle, Jamie, Michelle, Marie, Nicole, Tracy, Stormy, and so many others. You guys are my tribe and I'm so thankful for you.

To *Holly Orrick, Misty Hodges, and Gemma Cameron*—fans and friends who won a chance to make an appearance in this book. I hope you all loved your characters. Holly, you were Reagan's best friend first, sister second. You kept her safe on the worst night of her life. Misty, your character was so fun to write. Without her, this story wouldn't have existed. I hope you enjoyed her! Gemma, your character was the perfect example of everything a mother should be. Though I don't plan it, most moms in my books don't turn out that well...so it was a breath of fresh air to tell your character's story.

To *my sister Kaitie*, for being my beta reader and book reporter. Thanks for putting up with my many, many questions.

As always, to *the FBI* for just ignoring my scary search history. I swear the crime scene clean-up searches were all for research.

To *my editor Sarah* for whipping this book into shape. Your kind words and amazing insights were invaluable.

To *Carla Kirkland*, an amazing teacher who has always believed in me. Talking to your English classes was something I will never forget!

To *the amazing bloggers* who signed up to help get Gunner in front of so many readers: you guys are my heroes!

And lastly, to *my readers*. Without you guys, I wouldn't be here. Gunner and Reagan's story needed to be told and it's because you guys believed in me that I was able to bring them to life. For every review, share, "like"; for everytime you tell a friend about my books or buy my latest work—thank you, thank you, thank you. My dreams come true with every book release and it's all because of you guys. I love you all!

If I have forgotten anyone, and I'm sure I have, please know it wasn't intentional. I am blessed with such amazing people in my corner. If you're reading this, I appreciate you.

ABOUT THE AUTHOR

KIERSTEN MODGLIN is an Amazon Top 10 bestselling author of psychological thrillers and a member of International Thriller Writers, Novelists, Inc., and the Alliance of Independent Authors. Kiersten is a KDP Select All-Star and a recipient of *ThrillerFix*'s Best Psychological Thriller Award, *Suspense Magazine*'s Best Book of 2021 Award, a 2022 Silver Falchion for Best Suspense, and a 2022 Silver Falchion for Best Overall Book of 2021. She grew up in rural western Kentucky and later relocated to Nashville, Tennessee, where she now lives with her husband, daughter, and their two Boston terriers: Cedric and Georgie. Kiersten's work is currently being translated into multiple languages and readers across the world refer to her as 'The Queen of Twists.' A Netflix addict, Shonda Rhimes superfan, psychology fanatic, and *indoor* enthusiast, Kiersten enjoys rainy days spent with her nose in a book.

Sign up for Kiersten's newsletter here:
kierstenmodglinauthor.com/nlsignup

Sign up for text alerts from Kiersten here:
kierstenmodglinauthor.com/textalerts

kierstenmodglinauthor.com
www.facebook.com/kierstenmodglinauthor
www.facebook.com/groups/kmodsquad
www.twitter.com/kmodglinauthor
www.instagram.com/kierstenmodglinauthor
www.tiktok.com/@kierstenmodglinauthor
www.goodreads.com/kierstenmodglinauthor
www.bookbub.com/authors/kiersten-modglin
www.amazon.com/author/kierstenmodglin

ALSO BY KIERSTEN MODGLIN

STANDALONE NOVELS

Becoming Mrs. Abbott

The List

The Missing Piece

Playing Jenna

The Beginning After

The Better Choice

The Good Neighbors

The Lucky Ones

I Said Yes

The Mother-in-Law

The Dream Job

The Nanny's Secret

The Liar's Wife

My Husband's Secret

The Perfect Getaway

The Roommate

The Missing

Just Married

Our Little Secret

Widow Falls

Missing Daughter

The Reunion

Tell Me the Truth

The Dinner Guests

If You're Reading This...

A Quiet Retreat

ARRANGEMENT TRILOGY

The Arrangement (Book 1)

The Amendment (Book 2)

The Atonement (Book 3)

THE MESSES SERIES

The Cleaner (The Messes, #1)

The Healer (The Messes, #2)

The Liar (The Messes, #3)

The Prisoner (The Messes, #4)

NOVELLAS

The Long Route: A Lover's Landing Novella

The Stranger in the Woods: A Crimson Falls Novella